THE BEGINNING
OF FOREVER

A SUNSHINE + ACE STORY

A.E. VALDEZ

FIRST EDITION

Cover Art by Emily J. Fontana

Cover Design by Covers in Color

www.aevaldez.com

For those who encourage me to chase my dreams.
You're my ace.

CHAPTER I

Harlow

"Another six months?" I feel the reality of the situation crushing me.

"Miss Shaw, we realize it's an inconvenience but—"

"Thank you. I'll be in touch." I rise from my seat as I feel the sting of tears in my eyes.

This is a total disaster. The day that is supposed to be a dream has turned into a nightmare. I hurry out of the office to my car. Getting in, I exhale, and let the tears fall. All the plans we had are now ruined. I slam my palm against the steering wheel.

None of this is what I wanted.

I would've married Acyn the day he proposed. Just us two, right there on the beach.

But we wanted our families to share these moments with us. Now I'm wondering if that was a good idea. All the plans have become overwhelming, and it's feeling like our wedding isn't really 'our' wedding anymore.

Instead of going back to my studio like I had planned, I head home. There was some work that I wanted to finish up, but I couldn't concentrate on it now even if I wanted to. I call my assistant to let her know I won't be back in today.

"How'd it go?" Priscilla answers.

"Every direction but right." I let out a sigh.

"Oh no, what happened?" she asks sympathetically.

"I'd rather not talk about it right now. I wanted to let you know I won't be back in the office today."

"Don't worry. I got you covered. I'll finish up what I can and leave the rest for you to go over tomorrow."

"Thank you, Priscilla. Enjoy the rest of your day."

"You try to do the same."

I end the call, breathing a little easier, knowing I have the rest of the day to myself. Vision & Vibe is thriving; I opened the studio almost a year ago. I had to hire an assistant a few months in because, after working with Celeste, my former boss, on her ad campaign, I was flooded with opportunities.

Shortly after that, Sevyn asked me to go with her to New York Fashion week. I couldn't say no to a trip to New York City and an opportunity to photograph the newest collections from elite designers. It turned into more than I could've imagined.

After fashion week, a designer saw a picture I posted on my Instagram of her work. She reached out to me and asked if I'd be willing to work on an upcoming photoshoot with her. I've learned to say yes when opportunities present themselves. It opened the gate for me to do freelance fashion photography. It gives me a needed change of pace from my day–to–day when I get to jet off to a fashion shoot.

I turn up the music, roll down the windows, and head home, hoping I can salvage the plans we had.

Acyn

I'm surprised to see Harlow's car already parked in the garage when I arrive home. Usually, she'll text or stop by the shop if she wraps things up early at the studio. As I enter the house, I hear "Under Pressure" by Queen and David Bowie playing and follow the music to the backyard.

Harlow's lying on a blanket in the grass with Six-Two-Six, our cat named after Stitch from *Lilo & Stitch*, resting on her chest while smoking a joint. I stand near her head and look down at her, blocking the sunlight from her face. She squints as she looks up at me.

"You're home." She exhales the smoke she was holding in.

"I am." I sit down next to her, and she moves to rest her head in my lap. "What's up?" I ask as she holds the joint up to me.

"Nothing," she shrugs, "just tired."

I take a pull of the joint, hold it in, and exhale before saying, "You're a terrible liar. What's wrong, Sunshine?"

She doesn't say anything for a moment and then sits up to face me with tears in her eyes.

"Harlow, you're freaking me out. What's—"

Her eyes don't meet mine. "I don't want this, Acyn."

"Want... what?" I ask as my heart jackhammers in my chest.

She finally looks at me. "The wedding."

There isn't enough air in the world for me to catch my breath. My whole body becomes rigid as I break out in a cold sweat and my heart stutters in my chest.

"You don't want to—"

Her eyes widen as she covers her mouth. "That came out wrong." She scoots closer to me and grabs my face. "I don't want this big ass wedding we have planned. I want you. You're stuck with me forever." Her lips meet mine, but I don't fully register the kiss.

I finally exhale as I clutch my chest. "For a few seconds there, I thought you didn't want to marry me, and I panicked. Kidnapping crossed my mind."

She doubles over with laughter. "I'm sorry. I knew that came out wrong. I'm just... frustrated with it all. It's been six months since you proposed. I would've married you that day without a second thought to colors, menus, and cake options."

Harlow has been trying her best to keep up with all the wedding plans. It's overwhelming, even for me, and I'm on the sidelines of it all. Now we have a little over a hundred and fifty people on the guest list, and we only care about handful of them. I guess that's what happens when you're the only boy in a family of girls who's finally getting married.

"I also got a call from the venue today." She picks at the grass.

"Oh yeah, about what?"

"Well..." She takes another hit of the joint. "The director wanted to meet to tell me they double–booked our wedding with someone else's.

I guess they had gotten a new system and things got messed up. It came down to a matter of who called first, and it wasn't us."

"So, what does that mean?"

Her shoulders sag. "It means we have to wait another six months, and all the invitations we sent out a few months ago are bullshit."

"Six months?" I scoff. "For their fuck up?"

"I know. I got up and left. There was nothing more to be said. I'm exhausted, Acyn. Months of planning, and for what?"

My jaw tenses. "It took them months to figure out their fuck up, and now we're having to pay for it?" I shake my head. "I'm gonna stop by there tomorrow. That's bullshit."

Harlow's eyes are alight with excitement. "I should rage with you right now, but seeing you all riled up does something to me."

I let out a rumble of laughter. "Focus, Sunshine."

"I am. I'm focused on you." She straddles my lap, wrapping her arms around my neck. "You're in my corner. That's all that matters."

"Always." I kiss her neck. "But we need to decide what we're going to do. Do you want to wait that long?"

"No." She shakes her head. "I don't even want all the people we've invited to be at our wedding."

"Me neither. Fuck it. Let's elope."

"Acyn, your mom would kill me." She groans. "She's more invested in this wedding than we are."

I wrap my arms around her waist. "Exactly. That's the problem. It isn't her wedding. It's ours. What do you want, Sunshine?"

She bites her bottom lip and looks away from me as she thinks. "To marry you." Her eyes meet mine. "That's it."

"So what's stopping us?" I pull her closer to me.

I've been down for elopement since I slid that ring on her finger. Harlow tries to meet others' expectations while I have a hard time finding a fuck to give about other people's feelings.

I'm fiercely loyal to my family, but Harlow is everything to me. The wedding plans are stressing her out, and I know she isn't enjoying it. There hasn't been a decision she's made without my mom's direct involvement. I love that they get along, but I think the essence of who Harlow is has gotten lost in all the plans.

"Acyn..."

"Sunshine, all I want is you. That's it. Fuck a guest list and expectations. It's us."

"Us." She smiles. "I'm all in."

There are no words left to be said. I pull her towards me until our lips meet. My hands roam over the familiar curves of her body. She moans into my mouth as she grinds herself against me. I slip my hand under her shirt and cup her breast while the other unfastens her jeans.

"Acyn..." She pulls away, but I pull her back to me and trail kisses down her neck. "Acyn, the neighbors."

"What about them?" I ask as she lets me pull her shirt over her head, her bra soon following.

"They'll—" She sharply inhales as I swirl my tongue around her taut nipple.

"Sorry. I didn't hear that." I smirk. "What did you say?"

She pushes me back. "They'll see us."

"Harlow, the Murphys are on vacation and Mrs. Brown is as blind as a bat. She thought Six-Two-Six was a dog, for fuck's sake." She giggles. "Now, if you'll excuse me. I'd like a taste of you." She squeals as I flip her onto her back, and I kiss her before sitting up to pull off her pants. She lifts her hips as I slide them down as she spreads her legs for me. Harlow is a masterpiece. I rake my fingers up her legs and over her stomach, appreciating the work of art she is and my art adorning her rich golden brown skin. Since her first tattoo with me, she's gotten more that are mostly in inconspicuous places that only I'll have the pleasure of seeing.

"Thought you didn't want to be fucked outside, Sunshine." I grab her ankle and pull her towards me. My dick is begging to be inside her as it presses against my jeans.

She simpers. "Stop talking shit and make me cum."

"With pleasure." I say, sinking between her legs. I kiss and nip at her thighs before pulling her panties to the side and slowly gliding my tongue along her pussy.

She drapes her legs over my shoulders and pushes my head into her center as she tries her best to hold back moans. I lick and suck on her clit as she hums with pleasure. Her body trembles as I dip my tongue inside her. I've been addicted to her since the first taste, and it's been one of my personal goals to make her come as often as possible since then. I've yet to miss an opportunity, which is why she's letting me eat her for lunch in our backyard. She arches her back and grips my curls. I loop my arms underneath her legs and use my hands to spread her thighs further apart.

I know she's about to cum from the way she's breathing heavily and grinding against my face as she teeters on the edge of her climax. I move my tongue in circles around her clit before sucking on it, causing her to unravel. She comes hard for me. Her cries reverberate around us, and there's no denying that every person on our block heard it. She claps her hand over her mouth as she continues to moan and tremble.

I stop sucking when her moans turn to satiated whimpers. The way she looks after coming, with hazy eyes hungry for me, is one of my favorite views. She sits up to unbuckle my belt and dips her hand in my boxers. Wrapping her fingers around my thick length, she squeezes as she pulls it out and then pumps her hands a few times, causing me to groan.

She lies back, opening her legs for me, and I push into her warmth. I let out a shuddering breath before I move my hips. She puts one leg over my shoulder as I grip her other thigh that's wrapped around my waist. I slowly pump in and out of her, watching my shaft become wet with her arousal.

"Goddamn, you're gonna be the death of me..."

"At least you'll die happy inside of me," she quips as she matches my thrusts.

She isn't wrong. I wrap my hand around her throat and pound into her as I feel the release I've been chasing steadily building in my core. Harlow looks like a goddess bathed in sunlight with sweat glistening off her rich golden brown skin and her hair splayed across the blanket. Just when I think she can't look or feel any better, her pussy tightens around me. Whoever discovered Kegels, I want to thank them because the way I'm about to bust, I may very well die. I desperately thrust into her as she squeezes her eyes shut and calls out my name.

"Ahh, fuck, Harlow..." I let out a harsh, throaty moan as my body momentarily tenses.

My release spills into her as my climax shivers through me. Harlow keeps moving her hips, determined to get every drop from me. Taking a sharp inhale of breath, I moan, reveling in the feel of her. I'm already thinking of round two when our neighbor interrupts my thoughts.

"Is Harlow alright, dear?" Mrs. Brown asks from the other side of the fence.

I collapse on top of Harlow to cover her up as she clasps a hand over her mouth and laughs hysterically. I'm still balls deep inside of her and the only thing she has on is her panties.

"Uh yeah... she's fine, Mrs. Brown. Thank you for asking." Harlow is laughing so hard I can see the tears in her eyes. I grin back at her as I shake my head.

"Are you sure? It sounded like a scream and—"

"I was laying pipe, Mrs. Brown." I respond.

Mrs. Brown gasps. "Oh no, did a pipe burst?"

Harlow is now silently wheezing with laughter.

"It sure did, but Harlow helped me fix it."

"She's a good girl, that one. I'm happy you two are getting married."

"She's a very good girl." I look into Harlow's eyes. "And she's mine." I add for only Harlow to hear.

"Well, I won't keep you. Tell Harlow I said hello."

"I will." I respond and then wait for the sound of her backdoor sliding shut.

Harlow laughs, shaking her head. "You fucking exhibitionist."

"Call me what you will." I chuckle. "I wanted you. Surroundings be damned."

She grabs for her shirt and then slips it over her head. "You can have me anywhere you want." Her lips meet mine.

"Unless you want to give Mrs. Brown another show, I suggest we go inside first."

"I really hope she is as blind as a bat, like you said."

"If she isn't, she got a nice view of my ass."

"Acyn!" Harlow cackles.

CHAPTER 2

Harlow

All the lights are off with candles lit and music playing in the background. Rain is pouring outside while Acyn lies next to me. It's the perfect time to plan our elopement. We decided that the best place for us to get married is the Oregon Coast. It's where we fell in love and he proposed to me—it's perfect. I wanted a beach wedding in the beginning, but with so many people involved in the planning process, it didn't turn out that way. I was nervous about eloping, but as we sit here and make plans together, I know in my heart this is perfect for us.

"What about this coming weekend?" I ask, while staring at my computer screen. "I don't need to go into the studio on Friday."

Acyn grabs his phone off the nightstand and opens his schedule. "Umm... that could work. I don't have any clients on Friday, so we could leave Thursday after we're done with work and head for the Coast. What day do you want to get married?"

My heart rate quickens as the corners of my mouth turn up. "This is actually happening?"

He looks at me. "This is actually fucking happening."

I squeal and throw myself at him. "I can't wait to officially call you my husband. Not that we need a piece of paper to prove that, but—"

"But it's what we want." He wraps his arms around me. "In a matter of days, you'll be Mrs. DeConto and stuck with me for the rest of your days."

"Happily stuck with you." I press a kiss to his lips before sitting up and grabbing my laptop. He sits up with me and drapes his arms over my shoulders. "We need to get an officiant, and I need to call my friend to see if she can go with us to the coast to take pictures. Thankfully, we already put in our marriage license application. I just need a dress, but I think I have that covered. We need to get you a tux. Do you have any ideas about what you want?"

We decided that we weren't going to use anything from the big ceremony. It would make it obvious what we're doing, and we want this to be ours.

"Believe it or not, I have a Pinterest board Sevyn helped me make."

I gape at him. "Truly the man of my dreams."

He chuckles. "I speak all your languages, babe."

"Okay, now let's pick an officiant. Hopefully we can find someone amazing on such short notice."

"We will," he assures me.

For the next hour, we search for an officiant and read reviews. Fortunately, there are a few who do elopements and are familiar with last-minute requests. I reach out to them while Acyn figures out where he's getting his tux.

"Alright, that's all done. This is a breeze compared to the months of planning we've endured."

"The best part is that you're happy, and that makes me happy."

I smile at him as I snap my laptop closed and snuggle up next to him. "Do you think our families will suspect anything?"

"Nah. We take trips together often enough that it shouldn't raise any suspicion that we're going to Oregon for the weekend."

We travel together a lot. Especially since I've been traveling more for photoshoots. He'll come with me if he can and sometimes even work with clients, depending on where we go.

"What are we going to do about the other ceremony?" I ask. "I still want to do the bachelor and bachelorette party in Vegas, and a reception would be fun to celebrate with people."

He rubs his hand up and down my arm. "We should chop the guest list down. I haven't seen half the people on my mom's list since I was a child."

"She wants people to see that her only son is getting married."

"Our love isn't a spectacle, Sunshine. It should be people who've been there for us."

"I agree." I snuggle closer to him. "We can go over the guest list together. Does that mean you still want to have the parties and the reception?"

"Yeah, Kyrell has put a lot into that bachelor party."

"I'm sure he has." I mutter, and he chuckles.

"Plus, it will be with people we actually want to be with. But the reception, I'm down for that if we comb through the guest list."

"How are we going to tell your mom?" I ask.

"Don't worry about her. I'm her favorite child. She'll be fine."

I toss my head back and laugh. "That's all the more reason for me to be concerned."

"This is about us, Sunshine. My only concern right now is making you my wife."

His words cause my worry to fade away as he brings his lips to mine.

My dad lives in a townhouse that isn't too far from us. His retirement didn't last long before he began working as an adjunct professor at the University of Washington. He loves it and can create his own schedule depending on how much he wants to work. After his heart attack, he did his best to become active and found a love for hiking. Acyn, West, and I join him on most hikes. Neither of us has been back to Texas since the move. It's been the best thing for us.

I find him in the kitchen making fish and chips. He recently went to the UK and has been determined to re-create what he tasted there.

"Hi, Dad." I kiss his cheek. "Do you need some help?"

"No, kiddo. Have a seat. I'm almost done."

"What are you doing on your Spring Break?" I pull off my mini Louis Vuitton backpack and set it next to me as I take a seat at the table.

"Umm..." he says distractedly, as he plates the food. "I think West and I may go camping for a night or two. You and Acyn are welcome to join us."

My dad and West have become closer since moving out here and have the brotherly bond he'd always longed for. It's been beautiful to watch them become best friends.

"We're actually planning to go to the coast this weekend, and our schedules are packed until then. Maybe we can plan something with the whole family this summer?"

He chuckles. "I don't know if Ava will be up for camping again."

The last time we went, Ava, my aunt, came across some poison ivy. She thought it was pretty and used it to make a flower crown. Unfortunately, none of us noticed until after she had it on for a few hours. Her rash lasted nearly two weeks, and she swore off camping after that.

"Maybe we can rent a nice cabin?"

"She may go for that." He sets a plate of fish and chips in front of me before taking his seat. "If not, maybe we can plan a nice vacation somewhere poison ivy-free."

I waste no time digging into my food. "I'm glad you took that trip to the UK. This may be one of my favorite meals."

"Thanks kiddo. What are you two planning to do while visiting the coast?"

"Just to visit and get away." I try to sound nonchalant.

"Are the wedding plans getting to you again?"

My dad knows how stressful planning the wedding has been for me. The weight I felt when the venue told us it would be six months before we could marry is gone. It left as soon as Acyn and I decided to elope.

"I actually wanted to ask you something."

"Yes?" he sets his fork down and looks at me expectantly.

"Would you mind if I altered mom's wedding dress a little? Just enough for it to properly fit me?"

His eyes glisten as he looks at me, and tears pool in my own. My dad gave me my mom's wedding dress when I was thirteen. It was a year after she passed and the first time either of us could bear touching her things. My dad thought it would be best to pack her stuff and keep it in storage because it was a constant reminder that she was no longer with us. We kept some things to remember her. My dad hadn't slept in their bed since the night she had passed. Instead, he stayed in the guest bedroom and left their bedroom frozen in time.

"She would've loved that. I would love that." He wipes tears from his eyes. "But didn't you, Gloria, and the girls already pick out a dress?"

A few weeks after Acyn proposed, I went on a trip with Gloria, Ava, Sevyn, and Acyn's two older sisters, Annalise and Nora, to shop for a wedding dress. I had wanted to wear my mom's wedding dress, but Gloria had suggested we at least look at other gowns. I found one that I love, but it doesn't have any meaning.

"Yeah, I did, but I want to wear mom's for some photos with Acyn."

"I can't wait to see them." He smiles.

I feel a momentary twinge of sadness for lying to my dad, but it's quickly soothed by the fact I know Acyn and I are doing what's best for us. My dad has only ever wanted the best for me.

Later that evening, I'm ringing Sevyn's doorbell. She's helping with alterations. I would've gone to another seamstress, but I trust her to handle my mom's dress with care. She can also get things done faster with only three more days to go.

She opens the door with a glass of wine in her hand. "You know you don't have to knock, right?"

"I don't know what you and Zane have going on. I don't want to intrude."

"Please, as if the twins would ever let us. It'd be great to fuck anywhere but in secret places or while they're asleep."

I snort with laughter. "Where are they, anyway? It's quiet."

"Zane went to his parent's house. Eli and Emery would never miss a chance to be spoiled."

"Smart kids, if you ask me." I follow her to her sewing room.

Sevyn began classes at the Fashion Institute of Technology to get her degree in fashion design. It's a year-long program that she'll graduate from in a few months. I'm proud of her for doing something that she is passionate about for herself. Over the past year, her sewing skills have improved. She never took it seriously until she started school. Her designs are amazing. I can't wait to do a photoshoot for her when she's ready.

"Alright!" She claps her hands together after finishing her glass of wine. "Show me this dress."

I hang the garment bag up on a hook and unzip it. Sevyn stands behind me and gasps when I pull the dress out of the bag.

"Harls, my God, this is gorgeous. I love that it's vintage." Her eyes glitter as she reaches out to touch the dress. "And no offense, but this is prettier than the dress you picked out."

"None taken." I smile because I know she's right.

"You have to wear this dress for the wedding, not just for pictures. It's not too late to change your mind."

I'm supposed to pick up the other wedding dress a couple of weeks from now. All those plans are currently up in the air. My only focus is marrying Acyn this weekend.

"Do you think you can alter it?"

She sucks her teeth. "Can I alter it? Is the sky blue? Strip and put it on. I'm dying to see you in it."

I take the dress and disappear behind the room divider and do as I'm told. It's a soft, romantic cream color off the shoulder dress with lantern style sleeves. The back has a corset closure. After the alterations, it will fit me like a glove. My mom was more endowed than me in the chest area. It has a snug-fitting, heart-shaped bodice, but there's a gap when I put it on. The rest of the dress is flowy, gorgeous tulle. The sides need to be brought in just a stitch as well, and whatever else Sevyn thinks will make me look like a dream.

I step out from behind the divider, and she gasps while covering her mouth with her hands.

"Harlow... Acyn is going to drool over you."

I giggle. "That's the plan."

"Hot damn, alright! Let me work." She holds out her hand to help me up on the platform she uses for alterations, then grabs her pins. "We'll bring the top in just a cinch to give you some cleavage. The beadwork on the bodice is breathtaking. And then I'll also bring in the sides so it hugs your waist. Do you want me to make the bottom a little shorter, or do you want it to flow behind you?"

"Leave it."

"Good call. I think you'll lose the romantic feel of it, but wanted to ask anyway." She stands back, turning her head from side to side. "It honestly doesn't need much work. Do you want me to do it now?"

I blink, not realizing how minor the alterations were. "Yeah... if you have time. I don't want to rush you."

"No rush. Let me do it now while I'm free of the little tyrants."

"Alright." I chuckle before stepping down to put my clothes back on.

Sevyn takes the dress from me and begins working her magic. I send a text to Acyn to let him know I'm gonna be a bit longer.

Harlow: Sevyn is going to do the alterations now.

Acyn: Alright. I paid the officiant. We're officially getting married on Friday.

I let out a squeal, and Sevyn's eyes snap to mine. "What are you squealing about?"

"Nothing." I grin. "Just something Acyn said."

She shakes her head. "You two are nasty."

I toss my head back and laugh. "Who said it was sex related?"

"It may not be, but I'd rather not know." She mutters around the pins hanging out of her mouth.

"Oh please, what about all the S.O.S. texts you send me to watch Eli and Emery so you and Zane can fuck each other's brains out?"

Sevyn doesn't think I know that date nights are code for them to have an empty house to do whatever they want. Acyn and I don't mind, though.

She doubles over with laughter. "Just wait until you and Acyn have kids."

"I'm not worried." I shrug. "I'll just drop them off with you."

She smiles. "I'm happy you're gonna be my sister-in-law, Harlow."

Without Sevyn, I don't think Acyn and I would've met. We became friends when we met at a yoga class. At that time, I was working at the yoga studio and my Uncle West's coffee shop. She brought him to the shop with her and we went from friends to falling in love with each other.

"I'm happy too, babe."

"Okay." Sevyn sighs a few hours later. "This should fit you like a glove, babe." She hands the dress back to me. "Try it on."

I disappear behind the room divider for a second time. As I pull on the dress, I know she's right. It fits me perfectly. "Can you help me with the corset?"

"Of course." She says, cinching it snugly, giving my breasts a boost, before tying the bow at the bottom. "Oof, girl! You are perfection." She grabs my shoulders, turning me to face the mirror.

I'm stunned when I see myself. I look like I belong in a fairytale. The only thing I can do is stare at my reflection as Sevyn smiles beside me.

"Damn, I'm good." She flips her hair over her shoulder.

I chuckle, but I feel a tightness in my chest as I run my hands over the soft fabric of the dress. Tears prick my eyes. I try to blink them away, but that causes them to fall down my cheeks.

"Hey..." Sevyn says softly, wiping my tears away. "Are you okay?"

I nod, trying to control them, but they keep falling. "I just wish she were here, Sev. It isn't fair that she has to miss all of this."

She wraps me in a tight hug. "It isn't fair, and it fucking sucks."

I hug her tighter, grateful that she doesn't talk me out of the pain I'm feeling right now. Sometimes I just need to miss my mom while wrapped up in a hug from someone I love.

CHAPTER 3

Acyn

S ince Greyson and Asher are in town, I drag them along with me to get my tux. Greyson protested, but I reminded him how I endured ring shopping for hours so he could propose to his girlfriend, now fiancé, Selene. Asher enjoys spending money and wouldn't miss a chance to buy a new Armani suit, even though he doesn't need one.

I've never been one to follow tradition or rules. After asking Kyrell to be my best man, I asked Grey and Ash to be best men, too. Kyrell's only request was that he get to plan the bachelor party. I sent him a text Sunday night when Harlow and I were making plans to tell him I'd be tux shopping on Wednesday afternoon. He said he'd try to come. With a baby on the way and opening a second dispensary, he has a lot on his plate. This morning he sent me a text that he'd just touched down with Quinn and to send him the address of the tux shop.

Ash is already inside, getting tailored for a suit when I arrive. I chuckle and shake my head.

"Is this shopping trip for me or you?"

"We can have our cake and eat it too, Ace." He winks.

Grey is right behind me, followed by Kyrell. I give both of them a hug. We've created quite the "bromance" as Harlow calls it. She can call it what she will, but I know these three men will always have my back.

"Getting married, Ash?" Kyrell smirks.

"Fuck no," he replies. "I need to try all the flavors first."

"And you wonder why women never call you back," Grey says as he takes a seat.

"Who said I want them to?" Ash raises an eyebrow.

"You talk all that shit now until you go home to an empty house and a cold bed at night," I say as I look around.

Ash doesn't respond because he knows I'm right. All that partying shit is fun until it isn't.

"Whatever you want, I got it." Kyrell says. "Think of it as one of my gifts to you and Harlow."

"You don't have to—"

"I know," he interrupts, "but let me anyway."

"Alright." I smile and nod.

Kyrell is already paying for the bachelor party, including hotel rooms and flights. Harlow and I tried to talk him out of it, but there's no sense in arguing with him because he'll do it regardless of what we say.

"I would help, but this wedding Selene is planning is gonna run me a grip." Grey says, and he looks a little worried.

I feel for him because weddings aren't cheap. While both our families are covering the costs of the wedding, I still see all the receipts and am grateful they offered.

"You knew Selene was high maintenance before you asked her to marry you." Ash checks himself out in the mirror.

"Fuck off, Ash. You're the last person I'd ever take relationship advice from."

"A wedding is a whole different ballgame," I cut in. "Something you'll realize if you ever walk down the aisle, bruh." I clap Ash on the shoulder, and he rolls his eyes with a smirk.

"Mr. DeConto?" the tailor appears. "Right this way. My name is Mauricio, and I'll be helping you today."

He leads us back to a private fitting room and there's a bottle of bourbon with glasses sitting on the table waiting for us.

"Wow, Ace. This is fucking nice." Grey picks up the bottle of bourbon.

"You look like you could use a drink, Grey." Kyrell hands him a glass.

"Pour me one, too," Ash takes a seat, being cautious of his suit he's still wearing.

The tailor wheels in a wrack with the suits I wanted to try on. The one I was most intrigued by catches my eye immediately.

"Which would you like to try first?"

"This one." I point to the one with the floral jacket.

Mauricio smiles. "That's my favorite too. You have good taste."

Grey, Ash, and Kyrell enjoy the bourbon, engaged in conversation. Mauricio points me toward the dressing room. When I re-enter the fitting room, Kyrell whistles, and they all stop talking.

"For fuck's sake." I chuckle.

"That's a nice suit." Ash nods. "Never thought I'd dig floral, but here I am wishing I would've bought it first."

"Let me borrow that for my wedding after you're done with it." Grey jokes, but something tells me he's serious.

The blazer is slim-fitting with a silk lining. The exterior is black velvet with rich crimson and oxblood florals and deep forest green foliage. You can't really tell it's a floral pattern unless you're close to it. The colors are vibrant, yet moody and dark. The pants are a slim-fitting black that I'll pair with some loafers.

"That jacket is going to photograph well." Kyrell nods. "Harlow will be proud."

I'm sure Kyrell knows we're up to something, but he hasn't asked. If it were just for pictures, Harlow would be here to help me pick it out.

"A cream-colored button down would look nice underneath this." Mauricio suggests.

"I trust your judgment." I smooth my hand down the front.

He disappears for a few moments and returns with a cream-colored collarless dress shirt and black slacks. I try it on with the jacket and Mauricio was right. It pairs well. It's classy yet has the edge I want. I think it will match Harlow's dress nicely. I haven't seen it, but she told me it's vintage and romantic. A lot like her. It doesn't take Mauricio long to mark up where the adjustments need to be made. Once he's done, I change back into my clothes and hand him the jacket, shirt, and slacks.

"Just a few minor adjustments, Mr. DeConto. I'll have this ready no later than tomorrow morning."

"That's perfect." I shake his hand. "Thank you."

Ash heads back out to the dressing room to change out of his suit and purchase it. Grey gets a call from Selene and steps outside. Kyrell leans back against the armchair with a smile on his face.

"I know this is more than just a trip to the coast for pictures." He tips his glass back to finish the bourbon. "I've known Harlow too long. She's a terrible liar."

Kyrell has known Harlow longer than I have. They're best friends. I turn to him with a poker face and open my mouth to say something, but he holds up his hand as he sets his glass down on the table. He gets up and embraces me, and I hug him back.

"Her mom would've loved to see her this happy." He releases me without another word and exits the room.

I just finished up with my last client when Harlow comes walking through the door with two cups of coffee in her hands. I glance at the clock, not realizing how late it is. The last client's tattoo took longer than I had expected because they kept needing breaks.

"Thought I'd stop by to see if you could use some coffee." She hands it to me, then presses a kiss to my lips.

I wrap my arm around her waist, pulling her closer to me, and kiss her neck. "Thanks, Sunshine."

"How did tux shopping go?" She takes a seat on the bench near the window.

"Got a tux. I'll pick it up tomorrow morning."

"Were the guys any help?"

"I think Grey will start losing hair soon because of wedding plans."

She snorts with laughter. "Can you blame him?"

"No, I can't, actually. And Ash is Ash," I shrug. "I'm not sure if he fears commitment or truly is content with being a player for the rest of his life. Sometimes he just seems... lonely."

Ash gives all of us shit for being in committed relationships, but sometimes it seems like it bothers him.

"He probably is. His two best friends are getting married, and Kyrell is with Quinn and is gonna be a dad. If that were me, I'd feel as though I'm looking through a shop window. Everything is right there, but not really within reach."

"Damn Sunshine. You're getting deep."

She chuckles. "Are you worried about him?"

"No, but I don't want him to feel like he isn't a part of the group."

"Please," she sucks her teeth, rolling her eyes. "Ash probably thinks he is the group."

I let out a rumble of laughter. "He is a little egotistical."

"Little is putting it nicely, babe. I'm shocked Kyrell and Quinn made it on such short notice. Her showing up at the studio was a pleasant surprise." She smiles.

"I think Kyrell knows..."

"Knows what?"

"That we're eloping. He said you're a terrible liar. Which I already knew."

"Excuse me!" She laughs. "I am not!" I side eye her. "It's hard to lie to people I love, okay? Besides, my dad bought it."

"Really? That's your gauge? You could do no wrong in your dad's eyes."

"Aha!" She points her finger at me. "Sevyn believed me."

"True." I nod, shrugging. "I also think Kyrell knows you better than anyone aside from me."

"That he does. But did you tell him we were eloping?"

"No. He didn't give me a chance to say anything. Just said your mom would've loved to see you this happy."

She looks at me for a few breaths. "He said that?" Tears well in her eyes before she looks away again.

I sit next to her and pull her into my arms. The wedding amplified the reality that her mom isn't here to see us get married. Trying on her mother's wedding dress was the first time I realized how bittersweet this is for her.

"I'm sorry..." She sniffles.

"Never apologize for feeling the way you feel."

"I just really miss her. I mean... I miss her every day, but I've been missing her more than usual lately. She would've loved you."

"How could she not, Sunshine?"

"Really, Acyn?" She laughs hysterically.

"You said she would've loved me, and I really wanna know how she couldn't."

She shakes her head with a smile on her face and wipes the tears from her eyes. "The real question is, what would I do without you?"

I kiss her. "That's a question we'll never know the answer to because you'll never have to know."

The next morning, I pick up my tux on my way to work. I was half tempted to tell Harlow that we should skip work and head out to the coast instead, but I've never canceled on a client. I'm always consistent and honest. The luxury of owning my business is that I tailor my schedule to fit into my life. But there are days I want to say fuck it and do whatever the hell I want. Today is one of those days.

My phone buzzes with a text and the chime lets me know it's Harlow. She's had her own ringtone since the first night we "slept" together.

Sunshine: We should've skipped work today.

Ace: I had the same thought.

Sunshine: WE'RE GETTING MARRIED IN 24 HOURS!

Ace: Final-fucking-ly.

Sunshine: Dying of anticipation!

I'm typing out a text when a video call comes in from my mom.

"Hi, Mom."

"Hello, my love. I was trying to call Harlow, but she didn't answer."

"Oh, so I'm a last resort?"

Her shoulders shake with laughter. "No, no. Well... yes."

"The truth revealed." I chuckle.

My mom and Harlow are close. That is something I'm grateful for. I know my mom will never fill the void Harlow's mom left, but I think she at least makes that void a little less lonely.

"I was talking to Harlow earlier this week, and she said something about you two going out of town this weekend."

"Yeah, we leave tonight." Now I realize why Harlow didn't answer her call. She'd probably get nervous and tell her we're eloping.

"Where are you going?"

"The coast."

"Oh, Annalise and Nora are going to be in town this weekend. Maybe we should all go together."

I rub my eyes. "Mom, we wanted to get away. Just us two. Not have a family vacation."

"It wouldn't hurt to spend some time with your sisters, Acyn."

"And I will, when I want to." I smile.

"Alright. What are you two going to do there, anyway?"

"Harlow said something about engagement pictures and whatever else she wants to do."

"Isn't it a little late for engagement photos? Was she not happy with the ones you guys took?"

"Mom... I don't know. Whatever Harlow wants to do, I do." I shrug.

"As you should. Okay, well, I love you both and I'll see you when you get back."

"Love you, too."

I hang up and send a text to Harlow.

Ace: Avoiding my mom's calls?

Sunshine: She asks too many questions. We know I'm a terrible liar.

Ace: The worst.

Sunshine: Shut up.

My last client of the day walks through the front doors. A wave of excitement washes over me and I can't help the smile on my face. I get to marry the woman of my dreams soon.

The sun is setting as I load our bags into the back of my G-Wagon. I thought about taking the 1966 Mustang GT Harlow got me for my birthday, but I try not to push her, and the weather can be sketchy on the coast. Besides, Harlow over packed, as always.

"Funny you think you'll need clothes this weekend."

She wraps her arms around me. "Funny you think what's in those bags can be classified as clothing." She winks before kissing me.

I gape at her. "Now I want to see."

"Patience." She chuckles. "First we get married, then we do the freaky things."

"Wait... so what have we been doing this whole time? I thought you doing that little bendy thing you do is—"

"Make a PSA, won't you?" She swats at my chest.

"Pretty sure the way you call out my name is more than enough PSA for our neighbors." I smack her ass. "Now get that pretty ass of yours in this car so we can go."

"Yes, Zaddy!" She gives me a two-finger salute.

I chuckle and shake my head. I fucking love this woman.

Once I'm in the car, Harlow is ready to take pictures. I turn towards the camera with a cheesy, exaggerated smile.

"Why are you like this?" she laughs, shaking her head.

I wrap my arm around her neck and kiss her cheek as she snaps photos. She puts her phone down, places her hand over my heart, and kisses me.

"I love you."

"I love you, too." I kiss her again. "Onward into forever, Sunshine."

CHAPTER 4

Acyn

The coast is our place, giving us time to pause and just be. It always feels like coming home as we pull up to our little beach cottage we purchased together shortly after we got engaged. It's the same house we stayed in when I brought her to the Oregon Coast for the first time. Since I'd stayed here frequently over the years, I got to know the owners, Georgia and Joseph, pretty well. When they decided to sell, they reached out to me to see if I'd have any interest in buying it. They wanted it to go to someone they knew would appreciate it. We've already made countless memories here. It's where I realized I'd fallen for Harlow and then, a short while later, I proposed to her on the beach.

When I told her they offered us the house, we couldn't say no. It's a quaint three- bedroom, two-bath house that has everything we need for when we want to get away. Harlow's favorite part is the trail in the backyard that leads to a small private beach where we'll be getting married tomorrow.

"Who knew we'd eventually end up getting married here?" she asks as I park the car.

"I knew it was over for me when we took that first trip here." I cut the engine and we both get out. She meets me around the back of the car and leans against it while I grab our bags.

"That was a fun trip." She smiles.

"Even our swim in the Pacific?" I smirk, remembering when I threw us into the ocean.

"I could've easily died of hypothermia." She grabs the keys dangling from my pocket and opens the door.

"Nah." I kick the door shut behind me. "We would've been body to body before that happened."

"Damn." She turns on the lights as we head into the living room. "I feel I missed an opportunity."

I set the bags down. "We'll have countless opportunities now." I pull her into my arms. "How are we spending our last night as boyfriend and girlfriend?"

"Mmm... let's have dinner by the fire so we can eat under the stars. Maybe enjoy a joint or two. Then we can Netflix and chill, but we'll skip straight to the chill like we always do."

"That sounds perfect to me." I smile at her.

After we've settled in, Harlow makes us some blackened salmon and a side of Rasta pasta with shrimp in it.

"Taste it." She shoves a piece of shrimp in my face.

I open my mouth, and she puts it on my tongue. When she tries to pull her hand away, I catch her wrist and lick her fingers.

She giggles. "It's good then?"

"If I'm willing to lick it off you, it's good."

"I think the real question is, what wouldn't you lick off me?"

"Touché, Sunshine."

"Alright, you grab the drinks, and I'll take the food." She grabs the tray of food and heads out the backdoor. "Oh, and don't forget blankets!"

"Never forget the blankets." I chuckle as I grab the wine and glasses off the counter. Grabbing the blankets off the couch in the living room, I toss them over my shoulder and follow her outside.

She sets the food down on the table next to the fire that I started while she cooked.

"It's perfect tonight." She takes a deep breath, looking out at the ocean.

I watch her. I do that a lot—watch her do mundane things in total awe, appreciating being in her space. Although nothing with her is mundane. She lights up everything.

After we bought the house, she got all this stuff to have picnics on the beach. It's one of her favorite things to do when we come here. I should say one of *our* favorite things because I look forward to it too.

We settle on the blankets and pillows surrounding the low, candle-lit table and dig into our food.

Harlow moans as she takes a bite, and I chuckle. I like to think after a little over a year together that I'm used to it, but I'm not. My dick still twitches in response each time. It doesn't help that we're always trying to one up each other in the kitchen. We love to cook together and for each other. Either way, we're both winning because we make some bomb ass meals together.

"Are you happy we're eloping?" I put the last bite of food in my mouth.

She takes a sip of her wine. "Oh my God!" She exhales, placing a hand over her chest. "I am so happy. I felt like everything kept piling up. The venue, the never-ending guest list, all the pre-planning..." She takes a deep breath. "It was too much for me. Are you happy?"

"Of course." I give her a lopsided grin. "I didn't push elopement because I thought you were planning the wedding you wanted."

"It's not just my wedding, though. It's ours."

"Now it is." I smile at her as she goes back to eating her food.

Harlow could've said that we're skydiving into our wedding and I would've agreed. But I know her well enough to know that she wasn't happy with the wedding plans, long before the venue fucked up. She likes to make people happy, even if that means agreeing to shit that isn't really her.

"Are you nervous?" She sets her empty plate aside.

"Nah, I've been ready. Why? Are you?"

"No." She smiles. "I'm excited and happy because this," she motions between us, "is all I've wanted."

I've never felt the connection we have with anyone else. Even when we were just friends, the bond we shared was deep. We're on our own wavelength. I didn't believe in soul mates until her soul whispered to mine.

"You'll always be all I ever need."

Instead of going back inside once we're done eating, we sit on the beach talking and finish the bottle of wine. Harlow sits between my legs, wrapped up in my arms.

"We should probably get to bed. I need my beauty rest to marry you tomorrow."

"The moon and all the stars in the sky could never rival your beauty, Sunshine."

She sits up to turn around to face me, resting her hands on my legs. "So, how do you feel about immediately having babies?"

I put my hand behind her neck and pull her towards me, pressing my lips to hers. "A little one of us running around? Sounds like a shit show I'd love to be a part of."

Surprisingly, I'm awake before Harlow. We found it hard to fall asleep last night because our wedding day started with the sunrise. It's still surreal to me we're getting married. I doubt it'll ever stop feeling like a dream. I press a kiss to her cheek, to her forehead, and then one to her lips. She opens her eyes slowly, then closes them again. I chuckle, giving her another kiss.

"Why are you awake?" Her eyes are still closed.

"Because it's our wedding day, Sunshine."

Her eyes snap open as she springs upright. "It's our wedding day! Oh my God, we're getting married!" She squeals, throwing her arms around my neck and rains kisses all over my face. "You're gonna be my husband!"

"Yes," I say between kisses, "I am. And," she kisses me again, "you're," kiss, kiss, "gonna be," kiss, "my wife."

She kisses my neck and continues trailing kisses over my chest and abs. Sitting up, she rubs her hand over my morning wood before pulling my boxers down. I keep my eyes trained on her. I inhale sharply as she firmly wraps one hand around me and rubs the precum around the tip with the other, making it glisten. Her eyes meet mine as she slowly licks it off and then spits on it before rubbing it down my entire shaft.

"Shit..." I grunt.

She licks me from root to tip before taking me in her mouth. Her sucks are slow and hard. I brush her curls out of her face before gripping them tightly in my hand. I guide her up and down my dick, watching her with hungry eyes.

"Fuck, you look so good sucking on me." I groan.

She removes her hand that's wrapped around me and takes me further into her mouth. I fist her curls a little tighter. She rests one hand on my thigh while the other massages my balls. My head tips back and my eyes drift shut as I bask in the sensations.

She grips my dick again and sucks on the tip while still massaging me. I look back down at her as she swirls her tongue around the head. My breaths are shallow and sweat breaks out across my skin as she picks up the pace. I'm close to toppling over the edge.

I thrust into her mouth to match her sucks. "Fuck, suck me harder," I order her through gritted teeth. She sucks so hard my breath gets caught in my throat.

"I'm gonna fucking cum..." I pull her hair tighter.

A few more sucks and my muscles contract before I spill into her mouth. My hips stutter to a halt, but she keeps sucking on me until she's had her fill. She sits up and licks her lips with a smile on her face.

"Good morning to you, too." I say hoarsely and let my head fall back against the pillow. "I'm just gonna lie here for a minute."

She presses her lips to mine. "Wore you out? Gather your strength, Husband."

I open one eye to look at her. "Are you taunting me?"

"Me?" She splays her hand across her chest. "I would never. If I wore you out I–"

I'm off the bed and flipping her over my shoulder before she can finish her sentence. I smack her ass, and she yelps.

"Ace!" She giggles.

"You know I'll gladly fuck you into oblivion. Let me give you a preview of what you have to look forward to for the rest of your life." I hold her waist as I carry her into the shower.

Harlow grabs my arm to slip off her boots after our hike. We didn't want to spend the day sitting around just waiting. So, we went crabbing, then took a hike that ended with me fucking her up against a tree.

"I think I have bark in my panties. Words I never thought I'd say."

"I told you to take them off."

"Yeah? And what? Have my ass out if other hikers were to come along?"

I double over with laughter. "I'm not sure how having your panties pulled to the side is any better than having them off. Your ass is still out either way."

She tosses her hair over her shoulder with a smirk on her lips. "Look, it was worth it. But the couple we passed looked at us funny."

"You're loud." I shrug, slipping off my boots and unlocking the door.

"I love how you blame me when you started this exhibitionist bullshit."

I grab her as she walks through the door, wrap my arms around her waist, and kiss her. "Last I checked, you are a very willing participant, Sunshine."

"Always." She stands on her tiptoes and presses her lips to mine again. "But now..." she boops my nose with her fingertip, "I have to get ready to marry you."

"Did you just... boop me?" I quirk an eyebrow.

"Yes." She smiles and does it again. "Yes, I did."

I catch her wrist and pull her towards me. She squeals as I kiss her neck.

"Ace! I have to get ready, dammit. You've fucked me enough!"

"Oh, now you suddenly don't have shit to say? Where was all that energy from this morning?" She's too busy laughing to say anything. I hold on to her to keep her from falling over onto the floor. I make my voice high pitched and mimic her. "Wore you out, huh? Gather your strength, Husband? You better gather your strength, Wife, because as soon as we say I do, that bed upstairs is our home until we leave."

"Ohhh," she moans, "I love it when you talk dirty to me." She kisses me.

"Yeah," I nod. "We definitely belong together."

She snorts with laughter. "Okay, I seriously have to get ready now."

"Alright." I let her go.

"Do not enter the room, got it?" She narrows her eyes while poking her finger into my chest.

"Got it." I raise my hands up.

"See you soon." She kisses me again before turning and heading up the stairs.

I watch her and let out an exhale when I hear the door close behind her. I wasn't nervous until she said she had to get ready. It's a mix of both excitement and nervousness. The moment that once seemed so distant is now only a few hours away.

An hour and a half later, I'm putting on my suit. The photographer, Raven, who is also Harlow's friend, arrived early to help her with her hair and to take pictures of us while we get ready. At first, I thought it was ridiculous Harlow didn't want us to get ready together, but I'm glad we didn't. I can't wait to see her.

Once Raven's satisfied with her pictures, she heads back to the guest bedroom to help Harlow with her dress.

"Tell Harlow I'm heading outside," I say before she leaves the room.

"I will." Raven smiles. "She's almost ready. Just a few more details with her dress, then she's all yours."

My heart pounds in my chest as she leaves me alone again. I look at myself one last time in the mirror before grabbing my phone and sending a text to Georgia. I asked her to help me with a surprise for Harlow that she'll take care of while we're getting married. Opening the door, I set my phone on the dresser and head down the stairs. The officiant pulls up as I step outside. She waves and smiles from her car before getting out and heading toward me. She isn't very tall with warm brown eyes and is about the same age as my mom with short, white hair that falls to her chin with deep brown skin.

"Hi, I'm Sylvia. You must be the groom, Acyn." She extends her hand toward me.

"That's me." I smile. "I can walk you down to the beach. I'm waiting for my bride. She's still getting ready."

"Oh, no, no. That's unnecessary. If you point me in the right direction, I can find my way. Don't want to leave the bride waiting." She winks.

"Alright." I chuckle and point to the gate in the backyard. "If you follow the path just beyond the gate, it'll take you right to the beach."

"Perfect. I'll see you down there. Nice tux, by the way." She pats my arm.

Harlow is great at reading people. When we found Sylvia's website online, she said that she was the one who was going to marry us because of her energy. Everything is about energy to Harlow. All I know is she's never been wrong.

I head to the back gate and wait for Harlow to come outside. Now that Sylvia's gone, my heart returns to pounding in my chest. I've never been this nervous in my life. I try to focus on something else, but the only thing on my mind is Harlow.

Then, as if she heard my thoughts, I hear the backdoor open and slowly turn to see her.

I couldn't tell you the last time I cried, but when I see Harlow coming down the steps, she steals my breath and I feel a lump in my throat. She is a vision. I'm choked up as I try to catch my breath watching her walk towards me. Her dress looks as though it's made for her the way it hugs her breasts and waist before cascading down the rest of her body. She has a crown of flowers sitting atop her light brown curls that are flowing down her back.

When she's near, I hold my hand out to her, and she places hers in mine. I bring it to my lips without taking my eyes off her. There are tears in her eyes. I gently wipe one away as I straighten up again.

"Sunshine, you look divine. You are breathtakingly gorgeous. I should know because I still can't fucking breathe." She laughs and smooths her hand down the lapel of my tux. I grab her hand, interlacing our fingers.

"Are you ready to become husband and wife?"

"I'm all yours." She smiles.

CHAPTER 5

Harlow

Acyn has always been strikingly handsome, but him in this tux ready to marry me has me speechless and overcome with emotion. I can't take my eyes off him. It's tailored to his muscular frame perfectly. A few buttons are undone, giving me a nice view of his tattooed chest. He leads us down the path to the officiant. The sun is barely setting as we near the beach. This day couldn't be any more perfect.

"Acyn..."

"Yeah, Sunshine?" He stops walking and looks at me.

"I love you, and I'm happy I get to walk into forever with you."

He brings his lips to mine. "I love you, too."

We continue to walk hand in hand down the path toward the officiant until she comes into view. There's no décor, only the breathtaking view of the Pacific Ocean behind us.

"And you must be Harlow." Sylvia extends her hand out to me. "You are stunning, my dear."

"Thank you." I smile.

"Shall we begin?"

We say, "Yes," in unison.

"Then let us begin."

Acyn and I face each other. His ember eyes meet mine and there's the fire in them that's always been alight for me. Sylvia begins the ceremony, but all I see is Acyn. Even though we were just friends at first, he's always loved me as I am and encourages me to never dim my light. I fall madly in love with him every day.

"Sunshine..." Acyn gently squeezes my hand.

"Yes?" I'm lost in his eyes.

"The vows."

"Oh!" I let go of one of his hands to pull the piece of paper that I wrote them on out of my cleavage. Acyn raises an eyebrow while trying to hold back a laugh. "What? My dress doesn't have pockets. May as well hold it close to my heart."

He turns his attention to Sylvia. "You see why I'm marrying this woman?"

"I can." Sylvia laughs.

"Okay." I unfold the paper with shaky hands. I have it memorized, but looking into his eyes, there's a high possibility I'll forget. I take a deep breath, and meet his gaze.

"Ace, I found a home in you. Wherever we are, as long as I'm with you, I will always be home. I promise you'll always know love because I've loved you across lifetimes and will fiercely love you in this one and beyond."

I refold the paper, and before I can tuck it back into my dress, he takes it from my hand and tucks it into his jacket pocket over his heart. He kisses my hand that's still in his and pulls out a piece of paper from his pocket. My heart rate quickens as I watch his hands unfold it. Our eyes meet again as his deep voice fills the space between us.

"Sunshine, there aren't enough words in any language to express how much I love you. It's indescribable, but I can make sure you feel it. With everything that I am, I promise to show you every day for the rest of my days how much I love you. You're the heartbeat in my chest and the blood in my veins."

His words settle deep in my heart, and I feel like I can't breathe. He refolds the paper, kisses it, and then slips it into the front of my dress over my heart. His touch causes me to shiver and have goose bumps. He winks at me before holding both of my hands, and then I'm lost in his eyes again. Sylvia resumes the ceremony. Acyn and I say "I do" to each other and Sylvia turns her attention to Acyn.

"Do you have the rings?"

He pulls them out of his pocket, handing me his while holding onto mine.

"Let these rings not only be a reminder of your promises to each other but also a symbol of your eternal love and devotion to one another. Acyn, take Harlow's ring, and repeat after me."

He holds my hand and repeats after her as he slides it on my finger.

"With this ring, I give you my heart, love, friendship, and devotion for the rest of my days. I am yours forever and always."

"Harlow, take Acyn's ring, and repeat after me."

I hold Acyn's hand as I repeat after her and slide his ring onto his finger.

"With this ring, I give you my heart, love, friendship, and devotion for the rest of my days. I am yours forever and always."

"Now, by the power vested in me, I now pronounce you husband and wife. Acyn, you may—"

Before the words are out of her mouth, Acyn pulls me towards him and his lips are on mine. I wrap my arms around his neck and get lost in the kiss with him.

"Finally," he mutters against my lips before kissing me again.

I feel like I'm high. Our love is the best drug.

He pulls away to thank Sylvia. She congratulates us before wrapping us in a hug, and then she leaves. Raven stays a little while longer to get more photos of us before she leaves. And then it's just us.

"C'mon, Sunshine." He grabs my hand, pulling me toward the house. "I intend to keep my promise of making that bed our home."

We're both laughing as we run up the steps. I reach out to rush through the door, but he sweeps me off my feet, causing me to squeal.

"Gotta carry my wife over the threshold." A smile lights up his face.

I wrap my arms around his neck and kiss him. He carries me inside the house and kicks the door shut behind us. I'm ready to get out of this dress and on top of him. He takes me straight to the bedroom, as promised, and sets me down gently on the bed.

He whispers against my lips, "Open your eyes, Sunshine."

I open my eyes and gasp. "This is—you did all of this?"

There are candles lit all over the room, casting a soft, warm glow. Sunflowers and red rose petals are scattered across the floor. A bucket with a bottle of champagne and two glasses are sitting atop the bedside table. Twinkle lights are wrapped around the bedposts and music is playing softly.

"Yes, well, no. It's my idea, but Georgia put it together while we were getting married."

"Acyn." My eyes meet his. "This is gorgeous! I–" Instead of telling him, I show him.

My lips crash into his, and I pull him on top of me.

"You don't wanna take pictures?"

"Not as badly as I want you inside me." I turn around and brush my curls to the side. "Unwrap me."

"My pleasure." He presses a kiss to my shoulder, then one to my neck, and another just behind my ear.

My body shivers with anticipation. I feel him slowly untie the bow at the bottom of the corset. He gently pulls at the ribbons, one by one, and my dress slips a little further down my breasts each time. With one last tug, my dress pools around my hips. He pulls me flush against him, my back to his chest, as he trails his hands up my body until he cups my breasts.

"You're the greatest gift." He massages my breasts and kisses my neck.

Sliding my dress the rest of the way off, he drapes it over the armchair after setting the paper with his vows on the nightstand.

"And absolute perfection." He wraps his arms around me.

I traded the traditional white lingerie for black lace crotchless panties with a matching garter belt that's cinched around my waist. It's clipped to garters wrapped around my thighs. I chose black, not only because it's sexier, but it's Acyn's favorite color, and I'll do anything to please him.

Running my hands over the intricate lace, I smile at him. "You like?"

He pulls me toward him, threading his fingers through my curls as he guides my mouth to his. Our tongues dance around each other as my heart beats wildly. I doubt this feeling of bliss will ever fade with him. We fall back onto the bed, and I moan into his mouth when I feel the stiffness in his pants pressing against me.

"Why are you still dressed?"

He chuckles as he kisses my neck. "I was too busy admiring you."

I help him push his jacket off his broad shoulders before my greedy hands pull at his shirt. A button snaps off.

"Fuck it," I mutter against his lips and rip it the rest of the way off.

The buttons scatter around the room. There are too many fucking layers between me and my husband. He's already unbuttoning his pants and pulls them down with his boxers. My eyes take in every inch of his perfectly sculpted tattooed body. He climbs on top of me, crashing his lips into mine. I wrap my arms around his neck as he flips us over. Straddling him, I sit up and run my hands along his chest and abs. He grips my hips and guides me to move up his body until I'm hovering over his face.

"You know what to do, Sunshine." He smacks my ass, and I moan. "Sit like a good girl."

I spread my thighs further apart and lower myself onto his waiting mouth. His warm tongue tastes my center. He wraps his arms around me and palms my ass. My hands grip the headboard as waves of pleasure pulse through my body with each swirl of his tongue. These crotchless panties were worth every goddamn dollar.

I can't seem to catch my breath with the way his tongue is making love to my clit. I spread my thighs as far as I can, sitting on his face like it's my throne. He squeezes and smacks my ass in response, and I let out a cry of pleasure. Reaching down, I grab a handful of his curls. His hands grip my hips as I ride his face. My moans grow louder as I feel my climax building. He keeps one hand on my hip while the other rubs my nipples. The pleasure he's giving me is pure ecstasy.

"Acyn..." I moan. "I'm gonna fucking–" my words get lost in my throat as I fall over the edge into oblivion.

A guttural cry spills from my lips, and I grip the headboard to keep from falling over. My body shakes and twitches as my orgasm takes over me. My cries turn to whimpers as he laps up my release.

I collapse next to him on the bed, attempting to catch my breath. Acyn kisses my neck as his hands roam over my body. His lips meet mine, and I lazily kiss him back, spent from my earth shattering orgasm.

"Oh, Sunshine..." he kisses my lips. "Don't tell me you're already tired." He runs his fingers over my sensitive clit, causing me to moan. "Because I'm nowhere near done with you."

A smile tugs at my lips. "If you felt the orgasm I just had..."

"I tasted it, and I want more." He kisses my neck. "Every single drop that sweet pussy of yours has to give me. I want it. You're officially my wife. Officially all mine, and I intend to show you how much I love you for the rest of my days." His fingers massage my clit in slow circles.

My body warms up for round two of what is going to be an endless night of lovemaking. Turning on my side, I press my ass against his erection. He takes a sharp inhale of breath as I reach around, grab his dick, and run the head along my slickness before guiding him inside me.

He slowly pushes into me, letting out a shuddering breath while gripping my hip. Slinging one leg over his, I open myself for him to go deeper, and our lips meet. I moan into his mouth as he thrusts into me from behind. He pulls nearly all the way out before thrusting back into me, causing me to lose my breath.

"Mmm... yes, I love when you give it to me like that."

Wrapping his hand around my throat, he applies just the right amount of pressure while hitting my g-spot with each thrust of his hips.

"You feel so fucking good," he breathes out before lightly grazing my ear with his teeth, causing me to shudder.

I feel myself teetering on the edge of another climax. He teases my clit with one hand while the other moves from my neck down to my breast. His lips kiss my neck as he rubs and rolls my nipples with his fingertips. The feel of him all over me and filling me up pushes me over the edge into another orgasm. I call out his name as he thrusts into me. I throw it back at him to match his thrusts.

"Yes, baby. Bounce on this fucking dick," he growls as he grips my curls.

A few thrusts later, he falls over the edge with me. His body momentarily tenses as he grunts and then moans, spilling into me. I roll my hips, sliding up and down his length as his climax shudders through him. Our bodies slow as we melt into each other and the euphoric high of our release. He tightly wraps his arms around me, and I trace my fingertips along his tattoos.

"Can we stay like this forever?" I whisper.

He kisses my shoulder. "Of course, we have forever now."

CHAPTER 6

Harlow

Our wedding couldn't have been any more perfect. We spent the weekend totally and utterly lost in each other. I know we kept joking about elopement, but now that we have, I realize it's what we were going to do all along.

It's Sunday morning and the first time I've worn anything since I had my wedding dress on Friday evening.

"Damn, you really didn't bring any clothes, did you?" His eyes and hands appreciate my lacy bodysuit, thigh-high stockings, and sheer robe.

"I told you, nothing in my suitcases truly classifies as clothing other than what I had on for the drive here and when we went hiking. I bought everything else with filthy thoughts of you in mind."

"Can I just have you for breakfast instead?" He kisses my neck as I flip a piece of French toast.

I turn around in his arms wrapped around my waist and kiss him. "I–" my stomach rumbles.

"Maybe we should eat?" he smirks. "Death by sex in the first few days of marriage isn't ideal."

I snort with laughter. "No, not when I'm trying to spend a lifetime with you."

He presses a kiss to my lips before unwrapping his arms from around me. "Do you need help with anything?"

"Nope. I got it." I flip the last piece of French toast on to a plate. "It's all done. Besides, I don't think I could wait for anything else to cook. I'm starving."

"I told you that bed would be our home, Sunshine."

"No complaints here. I am thoroughly loved and fucked at the same damn time."

He lets out a rumble of laughter. "As you should be."

I hand him his plate of French toast, bacon, and eggs with a cup of orange juice before sitting down to eat my own. We weren't completely confined to the bed the past couple of days, but sex was the higher priority. Being newlyweds added to the urgency of needing our bodies to be intertwined as often as possible. And we took full advantage.

The realization that we'll be leaving in a few hours causes another thought to enter my head.

"Do you think your mom is going to be mad?" I take another bite, chewing slowly.

Taking a drink of his orange juice, he shrugs. "Does it really matter? Would we have done things differently?"

"No, this has been a dream." I smile, feeling on top of the world with him.

"We can't make everyone happy, Sunshine. We did what's best for us. Even if she gets upset, it isn't going to change the fact that you're now my wife." He takes my hand and kisses it.

"You're the best husband." I lean across the table and kiss him. Getting up from my chair, I let out a sigh. "Guess we should pack, and I should put on some real clothes."

He smirks. "I'm not opposed to what you're wearing."

"If it were up to you, you'd have me running around with my ass out all the time."

"I love that ass." He smacks it, and I let out a squeal of laughter.

I push his plate to the side and sit on the table in front of him. "Does breakfast come with dessert?" I open my legs.

"It does when you're the option." He pulls my panties to the side.

His warm tongue meets my center, and I let my head fall back as he shows me I've always been his only option.

Acyn

We arrived home yesterday evening, and now I'm in a trance watching Harlow do her morning yoga routine. She widens her stance before bending forward, and my eyes focus on her ass as she rests her head on the mat. My eyes flit to hers when she giggles and shakes her head. My phone rings, interrupting my thoughts before I can say something dirty.

"Hey Sev. What's up?" I ask with my eyes still on Harlow, who has moved on to another pose.

"Eli and Emery want to know if they can go over to your house tonight?"

I tear my eyes away from Harlow. "Of course, my favorite niece and nephew can come over. Just them, or will you and Zane come too?"

"Don't let Annalise and Nora hear you say that."

We may be siblings, but that doesn't mean we're close. Annalise is eight years older than me, and Nora is eleven years older. Annalise and Nora are only three years apart, while me and Sevyn are one year apart. The age gap made it hard to relate when we were younger. Now that we're older, we spend more time together since they moved back to Washington State, but I'll never be as close to them as I am to Sevyn.

"Sev, I'm pretty sure they know your kids are my favorite. Do you guys want to stop by at 6ish? Because I know regardless of what time I tell you, you'll be late."

"You know me well." She chuckles. "Yeah, that sounds good. I'll bring drinks and dessert."

"Bet. See you later."

Sevyn, Zane, and the twins arrive fashionably late at 7:00. It worked out for Harlow and me because we were both running late with clients. Instead of cooking a meal, we picked up pizza on the way home.

Eli comes running through the door at full speed. "Uncle Ace, look!" He points at his arm.

I kneel in front of him and see there's a small spider tattoo on his forearm. And this is why her kids are my favorite.

I smile. "Sunshine, look at Eli's arm."

She gasps. "Oh my God! That's the coolest tattoo, Eli!"

He giggles and smiles at us both.

"Who gave you your first tattoo, little dude?"

He points at Sev. "Mommy gave it to me! But daddy said I can't get a real one like you until I'm older." He pouts and crosses his arms.

I chuckle and put my hand under his chin so his eyes meet mine. "Maybe Mommy and Daddy will let me use some ink pens and draw a full sleeve on you."

His eyes light up. "Yes!" He turns to face Sevyn and Zane. "Please, please, please," he begs.

They both laugh at his prayer hands, pouty lip, and puppy dog eyes. It's hard to say no to the kid.

Sevyn tilts her head to the side, studying Eli for a moment "I don't know, Zane. What do you think?"

Zane crosses his arms, scratching his chin. "We'll probably get a call from the school."

"Probably." Sev shrugs.

"But he'll be the most badass kid at preschool." Zane smiles. "I guess he can get one."

I laugh as Eli jumps in the air, clapping his hands with excitement before hugging me.

"I want one too!" Emery whines, not wanting to miss out on the action.

"Oh yeah, bug? What do you want?"

Her eyes tip up to the ceiling as she thinks. "Mmm... can I have a unicorn?"

"Whatever you want, I'll make it happen." I smile at her before rising to my feet and then look at Sev and Zane. "Yeah, you two will definitely get calls from the school after I'm done with them."

A little over an hour later, we've all eaten our fill of pizza, pasta, ice cream, and brownies. Harlow is running around outside with the twins while Zane watches a basketball game and Sevyn helps me clean up. She leans against the counter after taking out the trash, and I feel her eyes on me.

"You and Harlow seem… different."

I ignore her prying statement and continue to load the dishwasher.

"I didn't think it was possible, but you two seem… closer. More attached. What did you do to her while on that trip?"

"Do to her?" I chuckle as all the positions we were in flash through my mind.

"Yeah… there's something different, and I can't put my finger on it."

I close the dishwasher, start it, and turn to face her. "You're reaching, Sev. As always." I pat the top of her head.

She sucks her teeth, shoving my arm away. "I saw the way you looked at her the first time you two met. I knew then that there would be something more between you. And I have the same feeling that you two are hiding something. Is she knocked up?"

"With the way I nut inside her? Probably." I shrug and give her a lopsided grin. Sevyn gags, and I laugh. "Why does it matter to you what Harlow and I have going on, anyway?"

"Because…" she looks down at the ground before her eyes meet mine again. "You're my big brother, and I love to see you happy." She shrugs. "That's all."

Her words catch me off guard. I know Sevyn loves me, but we spend more time joking and talking shit than saying it.

I pull her into a hug. "Can you keep a fucking secret?"

"Oh my God!" She pulls away from the hug, covering her mouth with her hands. "Fuck, yes! Are you going to fucking tell me?"

I look her up and down before sucking my teeth. "Nah."

"You asshole!" She punches my arm.

I laugh as she chases me out into the backyard with Harlow and the twins.

"Babies, get Uncle Ace!" Sev yells.

And like two wild animals, they listen and attack me. Harlow falls over, laughing as one latches onto my leg and the other to my arm. It's all fun and games until Emery's razor–sharp baby teeth attempt to take a bite out of my thigh.

"She bit me!" I holler as I fall to the ground.

Eli pulls my hair, and Emery jumps on my back. Harlow and Sevyn are both on the ground in a fit of laughter. Zane comes out moments later as Eli gets ready to sink his teeth into my shoulder.

"Oh, no!" he yells, drawing their attention to him. "Uncle Ace is being attacked by baby zombies."

The twins immediately stick their tongues out and tilt their head to one side. I laugh hysterically at their expressions. Zane helps me up, and then we stand back-to-back while the twins make growling noises, ready to attack again.

"Do you think we'll make it out alive?" I ask Zane dramatically.

"I don't know, but we'll die trying."

"Get 'em!" Harlow yells to the twins, and they lunge at us.

The girls laugh while Zane and I pretend to fight for our life. It eventually ends with all of us laying on the grass, laughing, underneath the stars.

"I'm tired." Eli yawns.

"Me too. Being a zombie is hard." Emery adds.

We all laugh as Sevyn says, "That's our cue to go."

"Yeah, gotta get these kids to bed. Thanks for having us over," Zane says as he rises to his feet. "And helping me fight the baby zombie apocalypse."

I stand to give him a hug. "Anytime, man." I kneel to hug the twins. "Bye little zombies. See ya soon."

Then they hug Harlow before Zane scoops them up. Sevyn tries to give me a hug, but I put my arm out, so she runs into the heel of my hand with her forehead. Harlow snorts with laughter.

"You two are ridiculous." She shakes her head.

"Fuck you too then," Sevyn says to me before hugging Harlow and kissing her on the cheek. "Bye, babe. Call me when you're tired of this idiot."

"She won't." I wrap my arm around Harlow's neck, kissing her temple.

"I'll see you Thursday," Harlow says to Sevyn.

"Ha!" Sevyn says. "See, she's already planning to be tired of you." She flicks me off before following Zane into the house and out the front door.

Harlow smiles and sighs. "I love when they come over."

"Me too." I smile. "Sevyn knows something is up, though."

"Did you tell her?" Her eyes meet mine.

"Fuck no!" She tosses her head back with laughter. "To be honest, I like the fact only we know."

She stands on her tiptoes, her lips meeting mine. "Me too. And I'd like to keep it that way for as long as we can."

I wrap my arms around her waist, twirling her around as she laughs. It was on the tip of my tongue earlier when I talked to Sevyn, but there will come a time when we'll have to tell everyone else. It's not that I'm not excited to tell them. I would broadcast it publicly to the world if given the chance, but I want to soak it up with her first.

CHAPTER 7

Harlow

Acyn may call me Sunshine, but there are days I feel like a thunderstorm. Today is one of them. A photoshoot that was planned months ago was a disaster. Nothing went right. The clothing items needed for the shoot weren't delivered on time. When it finally arrived and the model dressed, she was being difficult and not listening to direction. Then before I could take more than a few pictures, she fainted because she hadn't eaten anything all day and had to be taken to the hospital. My client is expecting these photos tomorrow morning, and I am working with a handful of pictures when I had hoped to capture hundreds.

I know these were all things entirely out of my control, but I still feel responsible. I'm a recovering people pleaser and try to bend over backwards for people even if I know they will be understanding. Staring at my computer screen, I try my best to work with what little I have. I jump when a bag lands on my desk and I look up to see Acyn.

Pulling my earbuds out, I smile at him. "I didn't hear you come in."

"You didn't answer your phone. I figured you were in the zone and stopped to get some Chinese food. Thought I'd chill with you." He presses a kiss to my forehead.

I stretch in my seat. "I could use a break. Today was a day."

"What happened?"

"Where do I even begin?" I ask, shaking my head and reach for the bag of food.

"Do I need to punch someone?" He smirks.

I snort with laughter. "No, it's not that serious. It was one of those days where all the little things added up."

Acyn settles on the couch with his food. I pull the box containing sweet and sour chicken with white rice out of the bag. My stomach growls at the sight of it. I had to skip lunch which didn't help my annoyed mood when I'm hangry on top of it.

I take a bite and moan. "God, I fucking love you."

Acyn chuckles. "I'd hope so. Since we've been married for almost a month now."

"I know! Isn't it crazy how time flies?"

After we became friends, I told him he'd make some woman very happy one day. I didn't realize that woman would be me.

"So... another celebrity booked me." He grins.

I gasp. "What? Babe! That's amazing. Who is it?"

"Macklemore."

"Are you serious?" My food nearly slips from my hands. "He's Seattle royalty! This is major."

He smiles. "I know, so I was wondering if you'd be willing to take photos?"

"Seriously? You're asking me if I'd be willing to take photos of my husband tatting up a celebrity?"

"I know." He rubs the back of his neck like he always does when he's nervous. "But I still wanted to ask."

"I'm so fucking proud of you."

I've learned a lot from Acyn. Not just about love, but about running a successful business. He's the best at what he does, yet humble and always looking for ways to improve and keep moving forward.

"Thanks, Sunshine."

We eat, and I tell him about my stressful day. After getting some food in my stomach and Acyn's good news, my mood lightens considerably. I put the last bite into my mouth and glance back at my computer, dreading the work I have to finish. I'd rather be home snuggled up with him and Six-Two-Six.

"I think I'll take this home and finish it."

He throws the food boxes in the trash and sits on the couch again. "I don't mind waiting for you. We both know you're less likely to get work done at home."

I groan, knowing he's right. "It's not like I have a lot to finish up, anyway."

"Your call, Sunshine."

Either way, I have to finish editing these photos tonight to have them ready for my client tomorrow. I'm kicking myself for telling them I could do it despite the setback of the clothing not being on time.

"I'd rather be home." I've been at my studio since 6:00 a.m., and I'm over it.

"Alright, do you want me to grab anything?"

"Can you grab the bag over there?" I point to the table. "I'll get my laptop and then we can go."

He grabs the bag, cleaning up my organized chaos along the way. It's the little things he does that make me feel all warm and gushy. I love when he just stops by my studio to spend time with me. I hope that never changes as time goes by. We walk out to his car, hand in hand. Since we work within a few blocks of each other, we take one car unless our schedules don't sync up.

When we pull up to our house, I let out a sigh. A hot, relaxing bath is on my mind as we walk inside and Six-Two-Six meows at us for taking too long to get home.

"I'm taking a bath." I say, stripping off my clothes as I head for the bathroom.

"I'm going to feed Six-Two-Six before he calls animal protective services on us."

"It isn't even that late." I chuckle.

We're usually home by 6:00 most evenings, but we're an hour late. He's a spoiled cat who likes his routine. When I get into the bathroom, I decide to take a hot shower instead of a bath because the work I have waiting for me. Once the hot water hits my skin, I relax. Letting the steam swirl around me as I finally breathe after a long day.

After my shower, I put on one of Acyn's t-shirts and head out to the living room to join him and finish up work. I hear him speaking to someone as I draw closer. When I get to the living room, I see his mom sitting there.

"Hi Harlow," Gloria says.

I glance at Acyn, and the look on his face lets me know the bubble we've been in for the past month is about to pop.

"Hi..." I give her an awkward hug before sitting next to Acyn and covering my lap with a pillow. "I didn't know you were stopping by."

"Neither did I." She straightens in her seat. "But when I called the wedding venue today to schedule a final walk-through with Ava for decorations and seating... they informed me you canceled the venue weeks ago."

I shift in my seat because I suddenly feel like I'm in the principal's office. "Gloria, I can explain—"

"Mom..." Acyn says. "The venue canceled on us because they double booked our wedding. The next available date is six months away."

Gloria places her hand over her chest. "Oh, they didn't tell me that. Well, six months is workable. Gives me more time to plan the wedding."

"We're not waiting six months, Mom." Acyn says, holding my hand, and his eyes meet mine. "We didn't wait. We already got married."

"I'm sorry... what?" she asks, blinking rapidly.

"We already got married, Mom. Nearly a month ago... when we went to the Oregon coast."

A pregnant silence follows Acyn's admission as she stares between the two of us. He rubs his thumb along my hand in his to calm my nerves. I'm not sure how he's not freaking out right now. I chew on the thumbnail of my other hand while she stares at us in stunned silence.

"It's what we wanted," I say.

Acyn

Harlow's palm is sweating in mine. My mom never drops by unannounced, and I knew when I saw her, she was here about the wedding. She's still staring at us as if we betrayed her. I'll never regret marrying Harlow or the way we did it. Not even my mom can make me feel bad about that. I'm not so sure about Harlow, though.

"I'm disappointed in you both," my mom says after an eternity of silence.

"Mom–"

"Excuse me?" Harlow asks in a dangerously low tone.

My eyes snap to hers because I've only heard her use that tone one other time, and it's when I fucked up before we got together. She rarely gets mad, but when she does, it's palatable, like a storm coming. Everything shifts.

"You two ran off without zero consideration of others."

"Zero consideration?" Harlow's eyes narrow as she lets go of my hand, clasping her hands together as she takes a deep breath.

I hold my breath as I wait for her to speak. Whatever she's about to say will be heard whether my mom likes it or not.

"Gloria," she holds her hands in a prayer position in front of her face, taking steadying breaths. "I've done nothing but consider others for our wedding. *Our own wedding.*" Her voice rises in volume. "It is our choice," she motions between me and her, "how we wanted this to go. I was exhausted from all the planning for a wedding that neither of us wanted. But we're the ones with zero consideration? Why? Because we don't want two hundred people at our wedding? Acyn and I don't even know two hundred people we'd want at the wedding. So yeah, Gloria, I'm tired of considering others because all I've wanted since your son proposed to me is to marry him. And we did just that. I refuse to allow you to make us feel bad about it."

"After all the time I spent planning." My mom shakes her head with tears in her eyes. "What am I going to tell everyone?"

I momentarily felt bad for my mom until I realized she listened to none of what Harlow said. She's somehow made our wedding about herself. This is the first time I've had to experience it firsthand. Harlow's been dealing with this for the past six months. Makes me wish I would've asked her more about the wedding plans. Maybe she wouldn't have felt so overwhelmed.

"Gloria..." Harlow takes a deep breath. "You keep saying *I.* It isn't your wedding. It's *ours.* Mine and Acyn's."

My mom ignores Harlow, turning her attention to me. "Acyn, is this how you feel?"

I grab Harlow's hand. "Yeah, Mom. I wanted to marry her the moment I proposed. But we wanted to share it with you guys... not everyone you could think of to invite."

"Clearly you didn't want to share it with us bad enough if you left everyone out."

She's hurt. I get that, but she's making this all about herself and it's working every one of my goddamn nerves.

Harlow rises from her seat. "This isn't about you, Gloria. I'm not sure what else I can say to make you understand that." She turns to me. "I have work to do. There's nothing more for me to say. I will not sit here to be reprimanded like a child for something I'll never regret."

She walks out of the living room, leaving me alone with my mom. Once I hear a door shut, I turn my attention back to her.

"Acyn, I've never seen this side of Harlow before. Are you sure this is what you want? With her?" she asks, pointing down the hallway.

I get up from my seat. "Don't do that."

"What?" She shrugs. "I think it's a valid question."

I rub my eyes with the heels of my hands. "I get that you're hurt and upset, but you're not going to ever disrespect my wife. She has shown you nothing but respect. If you're questioning what Harlow and I have... then maybe you don't need to be in our lives. Maybe you shouldn't have been helping her plan the wedding in the first place."

"Acyn—"

I hold up my hand. "I'm not Annalise, Nora, or Sevyn, Mom. The guilt trip may work with them, but it won't for me. And for you to question my love for Harlow because you're angry..." I shake my head. "I think you should go because there truly is nothing good for me to say right now."

She looks at me, waiting for me to change my mind. When I say nothing, she grabs her bag, rises from her seat, and walks toward the front door. I follow behind her. She turns to look at me, opening her mouth, but closes it again and leaves. I lock the door behind her and rest my head against it before going to talk to Harlow.

I slowly open the office door to find her wrapped in a blanket with her computer resting in her lap and tears falling down her face. She doesn't look at me as I walk in but stops what she's doing as I sit next to her. I take her laptop and set it on the coffee table. Then I pull her into my arms and bury my face in her curls.

"I'm sorry, Acyn... I just couldn't hold it in."

"Don't apologize, Sunshine." I wipe the tears from her cheeks. "It's pretty fucking hot when you get mad."

She cackles. "Stop it!"

"I'm serious! I didn't take you down on the couch for obvious reasons, but... I sure as hell wanted to."

She covers her face with her hands. "You're ridiculous."

I gently tug on her arm to pull her hand away from her face. "Are you okay, though?"

She lets out an exasperated sigh. "I hate disappointing people. Especially your mom, and I love her, but I'm glad we got married. I wouldn't have wanted it any other way."

I softly kiss her lips once, twice, and then I pull her flush against me, claiming her mouth. She straddles my lap, and my hands caress her thighs, hips, and to my delight she doesn't have any panties on.

"Goddamn, and you had no panties on this whole time?"

"I wasn't expecting company and was hoping for some stress release."

"Let me help you." I say, pressing my thumb against her clit.

She spreads her legs further apart as she pulls her t-shirt off. I take a moment to appreciate the beauty that is her before leaning forward and taking her nipple into my mouth. A soft moan spills from her lips. I place my hand at the back of her neck and pull her towards me as our lips meet again. She reaches down to undo my belt, pulling my pants and boxers down. Wrapping her hand around my length, she lines the head up with her entrance and sits on me. She takes a sharp inhale of breath as I thrust the rest of the way into her.

Leaning back, she places her hands on my knees as she slowly moves up and down my shaft. She watches me disappear inside her with each wind of her hips. Her breasts bounce in my face as she moans, picking up the tempo. I rake my hand up her thigh before rubbing my thumb against her clit.

Her hips buck, and she lets out a sensuous cry. Sweat breaks out across her skin as she rides me, keeping one hand on my knee and using the other to grasp the back of my neck. Her pussy tightens around my dick as she nears her climax.

"Ah, fuck yes. I needed you inside me," she moans.

I smack her ass before gripping it as she bounces on my dick, desperate for release. Her moans grow louder.

"Acyn!" She gasps as her orgasm shivers through her.

I grip her ass cheeks as she rides me into my release, toppling over the edge after her.

"Jesus fucking Christ," I rasp, holding onto her.

I rest my head on her chest and hear her heart beating wildly. We stay entwined, hugging each other for a while before she pulls away, kissing my forehead and then my lips. I look up at her, and she threads her fingers through my curls.

"Just so you know... I'd fight your mama over you."

We crack up, but we also know we'd go to war for each other. And that's love.

CHAPTER 8

Acyn

N either of us have heard from my mom since she left our house a few nights ago. I thought maybe she would have told my sisters, but I've talked to and seen Sevyn since then, and she didn't say anything. Even when she hung out with Harlow, she didn't say anything to her either. I worried that my mom trying to guilt trip us would have an effect on Harlow, but she just walked into my shop with a smile on her face and two shitty cups of coffee in hand.

She kisses me as she hands me a cup. "Hey. Do you have time to talk for a minute?"

"I always have time for you and shitty coffee."

"Fuck you." She laughs.

"What did you wanna talk about, Sunshine?" I ask, sitting next to her on the bench in front of the window.

"I want to tell my dad we eloped."

"Okay, do you want to stop by his place after work?"

"Yes." She smiles. "And I hope it's a better reaction than your mom."

I shake my head. "I'm still not sure what to say about that. But I bet your dad will be happy."

Her watch chimes, and she glances at it. "I've gotta get back to the studio to set up for my next client."

"Alright." I stand and hold my hand out to her.

She takes it and looks up at me as she stands. "You're okay... right? After everything?"

I wrap my arms around her and press a kiss to her forehead. "I'm good, Sunshine. It's me and you. That's all that matters."

"You'd tell me if you weren't, right?"

"Sunshine..." I grab her face. "I'd tell you if I felt any other way, but I'm happy." I kiss her. "And I mean that. My mom will have to come to terms with the fact that we're married in her own time."

She smiles after a moment of searching my eyes. "I just wanted to check in and make sure you're good."

"It helps that my wife is fine as fuck." I grab a handful of her ass.

She tosses her head back and laughs. "Alright, husband. I better go before we give everyone a morning peep show."

I chuckle and kiss her neck. "I'll see you later."

My phone rings while I'm in the middle of a tattoo. After going to voicemail, it vibrates with a text. I check my phone when I'm done with my client.

Dad: Do you have time to meet up today?

I scratch my jaw, letting out a sigh. My dad and I have always been close. But I'm not sure I want a lecture from him.

Dad: Just to talk.

I look at the time and decide I could go for lunch right now.

Acyn: Sure, do you want to meet at Pike's Place?

Dad: My treat. See you there.

I chuckle, shaking my head as I grab my keys and head out to my car.

When I arrive, I see my dad waiting outside of Pike Place Chowder for me. He has on some khaki chino pants, a white button down, and some boat shoes. He has rich copper brown skin like me with graying curly hair, the same ember brown eyes as mine, but he wears glasses. My dad looks nowhere near his age. Even with his salt and pepper curls, we're often mistaken for brothers.

"How are you?" he asks with a smile before giving me a hug.

"Good. Hungry as hell."

He chuckles. "Let's eat."

I follow him inside. I order a bread bowl of smoked salmon chowder and my dad orders the New England chowder.

When we sit at the table, I ask, "How's your week been?" before digging into my bowl.

"Good." He shrugs. "I'm having mixed feelings about retiring early. Not sure what I'll do with myself once I do."

My dad has his own accounting firm. He's the reason I've done so well with my business, aside from having the discipline and drive. Everything I know, I've learned from him.

"What do you want to do?"

"I don't know." He shrugs. "That's the problem. I retire, then what?"

"You rest, Dad. Do whatever you want to do."

"The downtime will be nice. That's what makes it so appealing."

He put everything he had into his company, and it paid off in the long run. As any business owner knows, the first few years can be tough. When he opened his accounting firm, I was old enough to remember how stressed and exhausted he was. Regardless, he stuck with it and saw it through. Now, a little over twenty-five years later, he's built one of the top accounting firms in the state of Washington.

"How's Harlow?" he asks after a few beats of silence.

"She's doing good..." I take a sip of soda. "Mom told you what happened, didn't she?"

He nods, "She did."

"I don't need you being the peacekeeper, Dad. We–"

"I support you both. You and Harlow."

I lean forward, resting my forearms on the table. "Oh... I wasn't–well, I don't know what I was expecting, but it wasn't that."

He chuckles. "Acyn, all that matters is the love you two have for each other. I'm no love expert, but I've been married to your mom for thirty-two years. One thing I know for sure is that other people's opinions of what you and Harlow do or don't do—don't matter. If you worry about that, it will inevitably create problems in your relationship. What matters is that you confide in one another because, at the end of the day, it's about you two creating a life together. Remember, you're committed to each other—not everyone else."

I take a deep breath, considering his words. "Mom made it seem like we betrayed the whole family by getting married."

"Your mom lost sight of what mattered. I don't know if you knew this, but we eloped too. We didn't have the money for a wedding. Even a small one."

"No, I didn't. Wait," I narrow my eyes, "then why does she expect us to have this extravagant wedding? She should understand."

"She should, but you'll always want better for your children. Even if what you consider best doesn't align with what they want."

"We tried to explain to her... but all she kept talking about was the plans she made and what she would tell people. Even asked if I was sure about Harlow." My jaw ticks as I remember.

"She was out of line for that and knows that you two belong together. Your mom handled most of the planning for your sister's weddings too, and I think she was expecting the same thing with yours. But... you and Harlow are entirely different from them. I don't say that in a bad way." He smiles. "I mean that you two care about what matters and not so much for the glitz and glamour of a situation. I'm like that too, and your mom and I have butted heads in the past about it. Still do."

"She's not talking to you, is she?" I smirk.

"Nope. Absolutely not." He chuckles. "But this is something I will stand my ground on. I'm happy for you, Ace, and proud of the man you've become. I love you and Harlow so much.

I rub my eyes, trying not to cry. "Uh..." I clear my throat. "Thank you, Dad. I really needed to hear that."

"She'll come around," he says, finishing his bowl of chowder.

"I know." I let out a sigh. "Thanks for meeting up to talk with me and for lunch."

"Of course. Maybe we can do this more often now that I'll have time."

"Yeah, I'd love that."

Harlow stares out the car window, nervously chewing on her thumbnail as we drive to her dad's place. I knock it out of her mouth, and she snorts with laughter.

"What? I'm nervous. I can't help it. What if he's pissed or hurt? Maybe–"

"Can we see what happens when we get there?"

I have a hard time imagining Felix ever being upset or disappointed in Harlow. He's always been understanding and supportive of us. I could be wrong, though. Harlow is his only child, and I hope he doesn't see me running off with her to get married as disrespectful.

"I guess." She rests her head against the window, letting out a sigh.

I chuckle, taking her hand in mine. "It'll be fine, Sunshine."

We pull up to her dad's place twenty minutes later. As I park the car, she's taking deep breaths while motioning her hands up and down. I shake my head, cutting the engine, and let her do her thing.

"Are you ready... or do you want to meditate for a bit too?"

She smiles, rolling her eyes. "Yes..." She breathes deeply again, shaking out her arms. "I'm ready. I'm ready. I am ready!" She claps her hands together.

"Sunshine, we're telling your dad we got married. Not going into a heavyweight fight."

"Acyn!" She grips my arm. "What if he's mad?"

I shrug. "Then he's mad, but honestly, we'll never know if you keep amping yourself up like you're going into battle."

"Alright, alright." She unbuckles her seatbelt and gets out of the car.

"Thank fuck," I mutter under my breath.

I follow her into her dad's house. He gave both of us a key after he moved in so we could stop by whenever we wanted and care for it when he's traveling. He's sitting in his chair, watching a movie.

"Oh, you two are here already!" He glances at the clock. "I sat down to watch a bit of John Wick, and here I am on chapter two already."

"It's fine, Dad." Harlow kisses his cheek. "We can just order out. Make it easy."

He rises from his chair, giving us both a hug. "How have you been, Acyn?"

"Good. Are we still on for our rafting trip next weekend?"

"Wouldn't miss it." He pats me on the shoulder with a smile. "I think West is coming, too. Did you want to invite Rafael?"

"Yeah, I'll see what my dad says."

It will give him a chance to see that there's a lot to do instead of just sitting at home after he retires. Harlow's palm is sweating in mine. I nudge her shoulder, giving her a reassuring smile.

"Do you want me to tell him?" I ask once he's out of earshot.

"No." She shakes her head. "I can do it."

"Rip that shit off like a band-aid, Sunshine." I wink at her.

She takes a deep breath as she heads to the kitchen to talk to her dad. He's leaning against the counter, going through a stack of paper restaurant menus.

"What do you kids want? I could always cook something too."

"Dad..."

"Yeah, Kiddo." He asks, distractedly. "Maybe Pho?"

"I–" she glances at me "–well, we have to tell you something."

He looks up from the menus and glances between the two of us. "Okay... what is it?"

"Acyn and I got married... about a month ago," she says all in one breath.

I glance between them both. Her dad takes off his glasses and rubs his eyes.

"Really?" he asks.

"Yeah..." she says. "We just—we wanted to get married and the wedding... it was becoming more than what either of us wanted, so... we eloped." She smiles, but it's a mix of a cringe and smile as she waits for his reply.

He sets his glasses and the menus on the counter and walks towards us. I hold my breath, not sure what he's going to do, but he wraps both of us in a hug.

"I am—" his voice cracks "—I am happy for you two. I just—God, Harlow. Your mom would have—she would have been just as happy and proud of you as I am." He holds onto us for a minute longer before letting go. "So, tell me all about it. How did it go? Did you wear your mother's dress?"

Harlow blinks. "You're not mad?"

He wipes his eyes with a paper towel he grabbed off the counter. "What? No. Why would I be?"

"It's just that..." her voice trails off.

I didn't expect her to be speechless. "My mom wasn't too happy about us eloping," I say.

Felix's face falls. "Oh, I'm sorry to hear that. What about Rafael?"

"I met up with my dad today. He's happy for us." I smile.

"You did?" Harlow asks.

"Yeah, you were too riddled with anxiety for me to bring it up on our drive over here."

She lets out a sigh, visibly relaxing. "This went so much better than all the scenarios I had imagined in my head."

I chuckle, pressing a kiss to her temple. "I tried to tell you."

"This is cause for a celebration." Felix smiles. "Why don't we go out to eat instead? Then you two can tell me all about it. I'd imagine you have an abundance of pictures."

"Oh!" She claps her hands together, looking at me. "Babe, can you run out and get the package on the backseat?"

"Yeah," I say.

She and her dad continue talking while I head outside. I hadn't even noticed she put a package on the backseat earlier. When I grab it, I realize it's a picture frame wrapped in navy blue paper with a gold ribbon around it.

"Here." I hand it to her.

She hands it to her dad. "This is for you. I'm sorry you weren't there, but—"

"Harlow, you don't have to apologize. Acyn asked me for your hand in marriage a couple of months before he proposed. I didn't have to be there to know that you're with who you were always meant to be with."

"Months?" she asks, looking at me.

"He didn't tell you?"

"No, I never knew." She looks at me expectantly.

"I asked him shortly after he moved here. My intentions have always been to marry you, Sunshine. It just took me awhile to find a ring, and once I found it, it was near my birthday... and I wanted you for my birthday so—"

She kisses me, wrapping her arms around my neck, and slipping her tongue into my mouth. The urge to fuck her on this counter is strong, but I remember this is her dad's house. I reluctantly pull away, clearing my throat and glancing at her dad. But he's not there anymore.

"Uh... your dad."

"Right. Sorry."

"No, I mean he's not here."

"Oh..." she turns around and then heads out to the living room to find him.

I follow behind her, and he's sitting on the couch, staring at the picture as he cries. When I get closer, I see it's of us at our wedding. Harlow looks stunning. Her dress is flowing behind her in the wind. My arms are wrapped tightly around her waist as I hold her up, and we're both laughing with her hands resting on my shoulders. That day was perfect.

"Harlow, you look like your mother... and you're wearing her dress. This is beautiful."

She sits next to her dad, hugging him. "Thank you, Dad."

Felix looks at me. "Get over here, Acyn. You're a part of the family, too."

We all laugh as I sit with them on the couch, and he wraps his arm around me and squeezes my shoulders. He looks at the photo for a minute longer before letting out a sigh.

"Alright, enough crying. Are you two ready to eat? I want to hear about this wedding." He rises to his feet, placing the picture on the mantle above his fireplace.

A few hours later, we've eaten our fill of food, and Harlow's face is alight with happiness as she tells her dad every detail about our wedding. I needed this as much as she did because I wish my mom could've been happy for us.

CHAPTER 9

Harlow

B efore heading home, I stop by Ava and West's house to pick up Mercy, their daughter. They have an event tonight, and I volunteered to watch her. Pulling up to their house makes me feel nostalgic. It was the first place I called home when I moved to Seattle, and it will always be special to me. Mercy's little face is peering through the window as I park, and she bounces with excitement when she sees me. I laugh and get out of the car. Ava opens the door as I walk up the steps with a smile on her face, holding Mercy in her arms.

"Harlow!" Mercy shouts. She has trouble pronouncing my name. It sounds more like Harls-Low, but she tries her best.

"My Mercy girl! How are you, sweet thing?" I ask as she launches herself into my arms.

"She's been waiting by the window since I told her you were coming to get her." Ava smiles, shutting the door behind me.

"Play, play, play." Mercy repeats as I follow Ava to the living room.

"Yes, we'll play. We've got to get your things first." I smile at her.

Ava grabs Mercy's diaper bag. "I think I have everything in here." She looks around the living room, seeing if she missed anything.

"Ava, we've got her. If she needs something, we'll get it, but she'll be fine. Don't stress."

"She's almost two, and I still feel like I don't know where my head is half the time."

I chuckle. "If it's any consolation, you're doing amazing."

She lets out a sigh, and her shoulders relax. "Thank you."

"Hey Harlow." West greets me, walking into the living room. "Thank you for watching Mercy." He kisses Mercy's cheek, and she giggles. "Cousin Harlow is here and nothing else matters, huh, babygirl?"

"Ready for the event tonight?" I ask him. West has been nominated for one of Seattle's prestigious business awards. Tonight, they find out if he won. Even if he doesn't, it's great exposure for his businesses, but awards are always nice.

"Born ready." He smiles. "Ava, you look stunning. Are you ready?"

"Thank you." She kisses West. "Almost. Just need to finish up my hair and a few details with my makeup. C'mon Harlow, we can catch up while I get ready."

I follow her to their room with Mercy in my arms. She won't let me put her down, and I'm okay with that. Ava and West's home makes you feel like you're stepping into a magazine. It's perfectly designed by Ava, but it has all the cozy vibes one would hope to have in a house.

She sits at her vanity, removing pins from her hair as she looks in the mirror. "So, tell me, how have you been?"

I sit on the chaise, and Mercy only gets down from my lap to play in Ava's makeup. "Um... good. I have something to tell you."

She whips around to face me. "Are you pregnant?"

"No." I laugh, shaking my head. "But Acyn and I eloped in Oregon a few weeks ago."

She gasps, covering her mouth with her hands. "Are you serious? Aw, that sounds so romantic! Was it romantic? The Oregon coast is so dreamy."

"Yes, to all your questions." I smile.

Ava gets up and wraps me in a hug. "I'm so happy for you." Her voice is shaky, and I can tell she has tears in her eyes. "You've grown into this amazing woman since you first moved here. I'm just so proud of you."

"Thanks Ava..." I blink back tears. "For all you and West have done for me."

"Of course." She pulls away, looking into my eyes. "We're always here, if you need anything at all." She touches my cheek, smiling at me warmly, before she sits back down at her vanity. "Who else knows? I'm assuming Felix."

I tuck my curls behind my ears. "Um... no one knew until after, but yes, my dad knows, and he's elated."

"Of course." She smiles, applying some blush to her cheeks.

"And..." I let out an exasperated sigh. "Gloria knows... she wasn't happy about the elopement. She's currently not talking to either Acyn or me."

She scoffs, rolling her eyes. "That's bullshit." Her eyes widen as she looks down at Mercy. I chuckle, but Mercy is too interested in her makeup box to care about what Ava is saying. "She should be happy for you both. This isn't a time for selfishness. What made you decide to elope?"

I tell Ava about the venue messing up the booking. "Acyn and I didn't want to wait. The wedding was becoming something bigger than what we wanted. You were there for the planning. It was a lot, right? Or am I wrong?"

"From what you wanted in the beginning and what it was turning into, yes, it was a lot. The venue refunded the money, right? If not, I can go down there and talk to them."

"Acyn went down the following day and got the money back."

"I love that man for you." She smiles at me in the mirror.

"Ava... what if I put a wedge in the relationship he has with his mom? Or the one she has... had... with me?"

"Uh uh, Harlow." She turns around, pointing her makeup brush at me. "You didn't. If anyone is putting a wedge in the relationship, it's her. Don't let how she feels overshadow this moment. Soak it up. Be happy. What you and Acyn do is you guy's business. You need permission from no one."

I take in her words, knowing she's right. "Thank you. I really needed to hear that."

She smiles, resuming touching up her makeup. "Be 100% honest with me. Was that venue what you truly wanted? Or were you going with it because Gloria raved about it?"

"Honestly, because Gloria raved about it." I shrug, looking down at my hands. "I'm a recovering people pleaser."

"I know, and that's okay. But when you feel you're doing something for the good of someone else, be sure to ask yourself if it's for the good of you, too."

Ava is the closest thing I have to a mother figure. I know I can talk to her about anything, and she'll be there for me without judgement. "I'll remember that."

"You are happy with the reception venue, right? If not, have no fear. I can work my magic, and we can find somewhere else."

"I love where we're having the reception. Sodo Park is gorgeous. We're lucky to even be having it there, thanks to you."

Sodo Park in downtown Seattle was at the top of my list for places to hold the reception. They offer everything for the event, from catering to décor if you need it. Since Ava is a well-known interior designer and event planner in Seattle, she secured the venue for us. I would be insane to change that. It's the one thing about the wedding I am excited about.

"Good." She messes with her hair a little more before sighing and saying, "I'm ready."

"You look gorgeous, Ava."

"Thank you." She smiles. "Alright Mercy, girl. Time to go."

Mercy looks at her makeup bag, at me, and then at Ava. I chuckle. "You can bring your makeup. We can give Acyn a makeover." She clutches her makeup bag to her chest and walks over to me. I pick her up. "Ready?" She gives me a toothy smile and nods her head. I turn to Ava. "Thank you for letting me vent and the reassurance."

"Always here." She slips on her heel before giving me a hug. "We'll meet up for brunch this week and go over the reception details. How does that sound?"

"Sounds perfect. Wave bye to mommy, Mercy." She waves. "We'll see you guys later tonight."

I'm breathing easier after talking to Ava. We don't need permission from anyone for what we do. It's unfortunate Gloria isn't as happy as we are, but I won't let that damper my happiness. I'm finally married to the man of my dreams. Nobody can tell me nothin'.

Our original wedding was supposed to be two months from today. We're sitting on our porch, listening to music while sharing a joint, as we comb over the guest list to trim it down. Even though we won't have the wedding, we still want to have a reception. It's been a little over a week since the fallout with his mom. After talking to his dad, mine, and Ava we've both been in better spirits. Her reaction didn't change our minds, but that doesn't mean it didn't hurt.

"From two hundred people to seventy-five. This is doable. There was no way in hell I was going to deal with two hundred people. In fact–" he grabs the list "–I think we can cut it down a little more."

"No, Ace!" I laugh, snatching it back from his hand. "If I leave it up to you, no one will be there but us."

"What's wrong with that?"

"Because..." I say, looking down at the guest list. "I still want to celebrate us with people we care about, you grump."

"I'll always be the cloud to your sunshine." He kisses my temple.

"I'm not sure why that sounds comforting and ominous at the same time."

He chuckles. "Comforting for you. Ominous for anyone who fucks with you. What are you gonna do this weekend while I'm gone?"

He's going on a whitewater rafting trip with both of our dads, Zane, and West.

"Oh, ya know, probably hire some male strippers, invite Sevyn over, and have a wild weekend. Since I'll be so fucking lonely." I smirk.

"Really?" He quirks an eyebrow.

"Uh huh, big, burly, oily, male strippers... all for me."

He gets up, rolling his shoulders before stretching his arms. "You want a show, Sunshine?"

"Oh my God, Acyn! No!" I look around because some of our neighbors are outside.

He changes the song on the speaker to Ginuwine's "Pony", turning it up causing some of our neighbors to look at our house. I'm laughing hysterically while also being mortified.

"Nah, you're gonna get a show."

"Acyn!" I whisper yell. "Stop! They're staring at us."

"Shit, they'll get a show, too."

I try to get up, but he straddles my lap, keeping me in place. I glance to the side to see Mrs. Murphy staring at us with her mouth open. I wave awkwardly as Acyn does a body roll. He thrusts his hips forward and the bulge in his gray sweatpants brushes against the side of my face. My eyes focus on his abs and dick that are now in front of me as my neighbors watch my husband give me a lap dance.

"Are you sure you weren't a stripper before this?" I ask through laughter.

"You said you wanted a stripper, so you're gonna get a fucking stripper."

He grabs the waist of his sweats to pull them off, and I grab his hands.

"Acyn, don't you fucking dare!"

He winks at me with his stupid, lopsided grin. Of course, he ignores me and pulls his damn sweats off. Mr. Murphy has now joined Mrs. Murphy on their lawn.

"Take it off, Acyn!" Mr. Murphy shouts, and then whistles.

Acyn gives him a nod and two-finger salute before he resumes his dancing.

"For fuck's sake!" I giggle, trying to sink down into my chair, but I can't because Acyn's straddling me again.

He's giving it his all with his body rolls and his hips that I know he can move so fucking well. Mrs. Brown steps out on her porch, wondering what all the commotion is. It's at this moment that I realize she isn't as blind as a bat as she stares at Acyn. This would be worse if he couldn't dance, but the man can fucking move. I'd stare too. I smack his ass as he turns around. If I had cash on me, I'd put it in his boxers.

"Alright, okay!" I cackle. "No male strippers! Just you!"

"That's what I fucking thought." He says cockily before flipping me over his shoulder in one fluid motion. "Thank you! I'll be performing same time next week." He shouts to our neighbors.

I can barely breathe from laughing so hard as he carries me inside.

I'm sitting cross-legged on Acyn's back as he does push-ups, scrolling through my phone. He leaves in a few hours for his weekend trip. We're sending out new invites today for the reception. Since it's so last minute, I think our guest list will be smaller than we expect. I know our closest friends will be there, but I'm not sure about extended family. His mom still hasn't talked to us.

"Babe..."

"Hm?" He grunts, pushing me up into the air.

"We have to tell Sevyn before we send out the new invites."

He does a few more push-ups before he lowers himself to the floor. I slide off his back, sitting next to him, and he rolls over to look at me.

"Yeah, you're right. I have to leave in a few hours. If you invite her over now, she should be here when I'm getting ready to walk out the door."

I snort with laughter. "You're not wrong. I'll text her now."

"Alright." He kisses my cheek. "I'm gonna take a shower and pack my shit."

A few hours later, Acyn is finishing up packing his things. In true Sevyn fashion, she shows up as Acyn is getting ready to load his bags in the car.

"Nice of you to show up." He smirks. "We have something we want to tell you."

She tosses her purse on the couch. "I knew it! What is it? Spill it!"

"If you'd stop talking, I would."

"Acyn..." I nudge his side. "Just tell her."

"Harlow and I got married when we went to the Oregon coast."

She gasps, covering her mouth. "I knew you two were up to something! That dress was too gorgeous just for engagement photos. Damn bro, you really said fuck everyone else. Does mom know?"

"She hasn't told you?" he asks.

"No. Why? What happened?"

"I've gotta go, but Harlow can fill you in."

I follow him outside and wait for him to put his bags in the car.

He turns to face me. "I'll see you when I get back. Don't party too hard with Sevyn."

I wrap my arms around him, hugging his middle. "Oh yeah, a real wild night of facemasks, food, and Netflix."

He grabs my chin, tipping my face towards his, and kisses me. "Love you, Sunshine. I'll call when I can. You know reception is shitty."

"Love you too." I kiss him again. "See you when you get back."

I head into the house once he's pulled out of the driveway. Sevyn has already poured us glasses of wine and has popcorn waiting in a bowl.

"Wasted no time." I laugh, plopping down next to her on the couch.

"Nope. Tell me what happened with mom. I need to know."

Letting out an exasperated sigh, I tell her everything. I decide to leave out Acyn talking to their dad because I felt that was personal for him.

"You know, when I got pregnant... she didn't talk to me for months." Sevyn admits.

"Months?" I ask incredulously.

She nods her head yes as she takes a sip of her wine. "She was upset because Zane and I hadn't been dating for long and we were young. Then we found out we were having twins. She thought my life was over. It was hard at first, but then I decided it didn't matter what she thought. I knew Zane loved me, and I wasn't going to allow her to steal our excitement. Nearly five years later and we have a beautiful life."

I hope it doesn't take Gloria months to come around. I'd like her to still be a part of things, just not managing them.

"It'll be alright, Harlow." She reassures me. "Give her time. She's gotten better now. It just takes her time to process things."

"Mmm... I guess I can understand that." I can't ignore the uneasy feeling I have in my stomach, despite her reassurance.

"Now, tell me every single detail about the wedding. Even the sex!"

"Sevyn!" I cackle. "I'm not telling you about our sex life. That's your brother!"

"I know all you two did was fuck after you said I do."

"Oh my God." I cover my face with my hands. "Why are you like this? You're Acyn in female form."

"That's why you love me so much." She smiles and scoots closer to me. "Now spill it!"

I tell Sevyn all the details of the wedding, minus the sexy ones, to her dismay. How she doesn't find that weird, I'll never know. But she helps me get the new invites ready and drop them off at the post office, so they hopefully reach people with enough time. After that, our night is as eventful as we hoped. Facemasks, drinks, food, laughter, and Netflix. The twins stayed with Zane's parents for the weekend so Sevyn could have some time to herself. Sevyn is like the sister I never had but hoped for. I always thank the universe that she walked into the yoga studio when she did, because that moment changed my life.

I slowly open my eyes to the morning's light and feel like I'm being assaulted. My whole body feels the two bottles of wine we drank last night. Sevyn has her leg draped over my body with her foot in my face. I don't even remember falling asleep on the couch last night. Glancing at the television, Netflix is asking if I'm still watching Queer Eye. I grab Sevyn's foot and move it off my chest to get up. Groggily stumbling into the kitchen, I grab a bottle of water from the fridge and lean against the counter as I gulp it down.

I hear my phone ringing somewhere in the house but don't remember where I had it last and follow the sound of it to the coffee table in the living room.

"Hello," I answer hoarsely.

"Damn, aren't you a sight to behold first thing in the morning?" Acyn asks as he appears on the screen.

I snort with laughter, rubbing my eyes. "I know I look like hell because I feel like it." Getting up from the couch, I head to the bathroom to find a Tylenol and make myself presentable even if I have no plans today. "How was your first night?"

"Good. West almost started a forest fire. Got a little too carried away with the lighter fluid."

I shake my head, laughing. "Leave it to West to do that."

Uncle West isn't necessarily clumsy, he's just overzealous. It makes for a fun time at his expense, though. I prop my phone up on the bathroom counter and continue talking to Acyn as I brush my teeth, wash my face, and pull my curls into a messy bun on the top of my head.

"What are you and Sevyn doing today?"

"I would like to say nothing, but we'll probably end up getting our nails done or something like that." When I return to the living room, she's still sleeping on the couch. "If she ever wakes up." I jump when I hear a knock on the door. It's too early for packages or visitors.

"Is that the male stripper?" Acyn asks as I head down the hallway to the front door.

"No, thanks to you. Our neighbors now whistle at me each time I go outside."

As I get closer to the door, I see an outline of someone in the glass and hope it isn't a Jehovah's witness.

He grins. "It was all worth it."

I peer through the glass and see Gloria. "Um... your mom's here. Can I call you back? Or wait, just call me when you're back from rafting if you have service."

"Are you sure you wanna answer that?"

"She knows I'm home, Acyn. Both mine and Sevyn's cars are parked in the driveway, and your dad's with you."

He lets out a sigh. "Alright, just—"

"I'll be fine." I smile at him. "Love you. Enjoy the trip. You'll know if we get into a knock down drag out fight."

He lets out a rumble of laughter. "You're all sunny and cute until you get pissed off. I'm not worried about you. I'm worried about her."

I roll my eyes with a smile tugging at my lips. "I've gotta answer the damn door. Bye. Love you."

"Love you too, Sunshine."

I hang up the phone, take a deep breath, and open the door.

"Gloria." I smile, despite my nervousness.

"Good morning, I hope I didn't wake you, but I was hoping we could talk."

"Of course." I step aside to let her in and close the door behind her. When we get to the living room, Sevyn is barely waking up.

She looks between me and Gloria. "Um... morning. I will... go get coffee or something to let you guys talk."

"Looks like you two had a fun night." Gloria says, surveying the bottles of wine and snack wrappers littering the coffee table.

"You know me, Mom." She kisses Gloria on the cheek. "I love a good time. I'll go get breakfast for us. Be back in a bit." Sevyn squeezes my hand as she walks past and gives me an encouraging smile.

"Do you want to sit outside?" I point to the backyard.

Acyn and I turned the deck into a small oasis. There is an abundance of plants, a couple of fountains, and plush seating.

"That sounds great."

We settle on the chairs outside. I shift in my seat, waiting for her to speak. A silence settles between us as she looks down at her hands before her eyes meet mine.

She takes a deep breath. "I want to apologize for the way things went the last time I was here. Even though it's tough for me to admit, I lost sight of what is truly important. That's the love you have for each other. I know you love my son just as much as I do... and so much more."

"We didn't—we didn't intend to cut anyone out, but the wedding... it just wasn't what we had envisioned for us."

"I know that now. Acyn has always been different, not just because he's the only boy, but because he's never cared for... the extra stuff. He likes the meat of things, not the garnish."

"Yeah." I nod my head with a smile. "That sums him up perfectly."

"The only time I've ever seen him care about the extra stuff is with his art and... you."

Tears sting my eyes. "Thank you, Gloria. That means a lot."

"I hope you can forgive me. I love you both so much."

I get up from my seat and hug her. "Of course."

I tried to not let her not talking to us get to me, but it did. Gloria is a mother figure to me and until we told her about the elopement, she had always been loving and inviting. Her reaction was a slap in the face. It stung, but I can also understand where she's coming from. I sit back down in my seat and smile at her.

"What do you two want to do?" she asks, wiping tears from her cheeks.

"We're still planning for the reception, but we cut the guest list down. Did you want to look at it?"

"No, no." She holds her hands up. "I'm simply here to support what you two want."

"Okay." I nod. "Would you like to see the photos from the wedding?" I ask.

"I'd love to." She smiles.

I disappear into the house and grab an album I made for her and Rafael.

"Here." I hand it to her as I sit down. "This is for you to keep."

She places her hand over her heart, looking down at the photo on the cover. It's the same one I gave to my dad.

"You can tell me what photos you'd like framed, and I'll do it for you."

"All of them." She replies.

I toss my head back with laughter. "I can do that too."

She grabs my hand and squeezes it. "I couldn't have asked for a better daughter-in-law."

CHAPTER 10

Acyn

I was relieved to hear that my mom apologized to Harlow. She invited us over for a family dinner tonight. I just got back from the whitewater rafting trip. I'm exhausted, but I'm looking forward to getting together with everyone. My mom also invited Felix, West, and Ava.

"Sunshine, are you almost ready?" I ask as I watch her apply lipstick in the mirror. "You talk about Sevyn, but..."

"First of all, we could be late, and we'll still arrive before them." She puts the cap back on her lipstick. "Serious question..." she says distractedly, as she looks at herself in the mirror.

"Yeah?"

"Do my titties look bigger?" She turns to face me and makes them bounce.

She's wearing a top that hugs them perfectly. It's hard to tell if it's the top, her making them bounce, if they really are bigger, or all of the above.

"I–this is a serious question? I mean, you're making them bounce in my face. How am I supposed to take this seriously?"

"Acyn, look at them," she says, squeezing them together with her hands.

"Oh, I am. And if you keep doing that, we'll never leave."

"Do they look bigger?" she says, making them bounce again.

I raise an eyebrow. "Do you want me to fuck you?"

She cracks up. "That's always a yes, but I really want to know if they look bigger, dammit. Turn your dick off your two seconds and focus."

"Turn my dick off? With you?" She gives me a look, and I clear my throat. "They look exactly like the titties I know and love."

"Huh..." she says while looking down at them. "I don't know. Maybe it's the top or this bra. Who knows, but I feel like they're bigger."

"If you want to take your top off so I could get a better look, I'd be happy to–"

"Nice try!" She laughs. "Let's go."

"Late for lipstick, but not for sex. Bullshit," I mutter as I follow her.

Harlow's sitting on the ground with Mercy in her lap. Emery is doing her hair, and Eli is telling her about his superhero action figures. Harlow isn't a fan of superheroes, but she's acting like they are the best thing in the world for Eli. The kids are always calm with her, but with me they act like I'm a human jungle gym. I have to admit, it's fun to toss them around and be a big kid.

Since Harlow's preoccupied and everyone else is in conversation, I step outside to watch the rainfall. It's nice to be hanging out with my family again. I complain about it, but it's something I enjoy. I hear the sliding glass door and turn to see my mom.

She loops her arm through mine. "You've always loved the rain. Even when you were a baby."

I smile at her. "It's calming."

"Acyn... I'm sorry for the things I said to you. And that I couldn't be happy for you in the moment."

I watch the rain, letting silence fall between us before I respond. "I've always been able to talk to you and dad about anything. For me to tell you about one of the most important moments of my life and then you question the love I have for the only woman I'll ever love... it didn't sit well with me. It still doesn't. Do you honestly question what we have?"

"You're my only son and—"

"That's no excuse, Mom. Whether I'm your only or fifth son, what you said... hurt. I never brought any women around you guys before Harlow because they didn't matter. But she... she's my heart. I know I may sound harsh right now, but I want you to know I won't tolerate you, or anyone else, ever questioning what we have."

She pats my arm and takes a few breaths before speaking. "I'm sorry I hurt you. I loved Harlow from the moment you brought her to that first dinner we had. She loves you as fiercely as you love her. I support you both, and I promise I won't plan anything else... unless asked."

I chuckle, feeling the tension I didn't know I had leave my body. "I love you, Mom."

"Love you, too." She says, resting her head against my arm as we watch the rain.

It's the day before we leave for our bachelor and bachelorette parties. Initially, we were going to have separate trips. But since Harlow's best friends, Quinn and Marisa, are planning the bachelorette party, Quinn suggested a joint trip to Las Vegas. We'll do some things together, but still have our separate parties and itineraries. I've been looking forward to this since Kyrell first told me he was going to throw it. Not because I want to get into fuckery, but because he knows how to have a good time. My phone chimes with a text, and Harlow tosses it in my direction from where she's sitting amongst our bags as she packs.

Kyrell: Are you ready to fucking party?

I laugh at his text, and Harlow narrows her eyes in my direction. She still isn't sure about the bachelor party, even though we'll be doing some stuff together. We're only going to be there for the weekend. We arrive early Friday afternoon. Saturday night is when we'll have our separate parties. Sunday is to recover from whatever happens Saturday, and then Monday morning we head back home.

Acyn: Hell yeah.

"You're cute when you're jealous, you know that?" I ask her.

"I'm not jealous. Why would I be jealous of a stripper who's paid to dance on you?"

"And the claws are out." I laugh. "Aren't you going to a strip show, anyway?"

"I am." She smiles smugly.

"Why are you jealous, then?"

"For the second time, I'm not jealous. I know you value your life too much to ever play with me. I also know you wouldn't do anything like that."

I sit down next to her on the floor and pull her into my arms. "Exactly, I never would." I kiss her. "But I'm gonna enjoy this fucking party."

"And I'll enjoy mine." She simpers.

"That sounds like a threat."

"It isn't." She shrugs. "I'm just looking forward to letting loose with the girls. It also means we're closer to getting to spend two entire weeks together on our honeymoon." She kisses me before sitting up again to finish packing her things.

We planned the honeymoon before we even thought about planning the wedding. Having time alone together after all the craziness was important for us. Since we both run our own businesses, we have to take into consideration the fact that we can't simply request time off. While we have people in place to manage things while we're gone, we still want to make sure everything is running smoothly so we can truly enjoy our time away together.

"We're almost there, Sunshine." I smile at her.

Our reception is next weekend, then we leave for our honeymoon. We'll be spending two weeks on an island called Seychelles that's off the east coast of Africa in the Indian ocean. I had never heard of it until she showed me pictures and I couldn't believe it existed. I don't give a damn where we go as long as I spend most of the honeymoon buried inside her.

Harlow

Being met by neon "Welcome to Las Vegas" lights as we step off the plane amps up my excitement for the weekend with my favorite people. We all tried to get flights as close to each other's arrival times as possible. Ace and I flew in with Sevyn and Zane. Kyrell and Quinn's flight should arrive in fifteen minutes. Marisa, Greyson, and Asher will meet us at the hotel in an hour.

Sevyn throws her arms over my shoulders and squeals. "Girl, this is gonna be a fun weekend."

I grin at her. "I know."

To be honest, I thought a Vegas bachelorette was cliché initially, but now that we're here, I know we won't run out of things to do. Acyn and Zane grab our luggage. I anxiously scan the crowd of people, trying to catch a glimpse of my two best friends.

"What time are they supposed to get here?" Acyn asks.

"Any—oh, there they are!" I hold on to his arm as I bounce up and down while waving at them. "Oh my God! Look at Quinn's baby bump."

I throw myself at Kyrell when they get closer, wrapping him in a hug. He picks me up off the ground, twirling me around.

"Missed you too, Harls," he says.

Once he sets me down, I squeeze Quinn in a tight hug. "You look fucking amazing, babe! You're glowing!"

"Thank you." She smiles. "I'm just happy to not be sick anymore."

Acyn gives Kyrell a hug. "Thanks again for setting this up for everyone."

"Don't mention it. Anything for you and Harls." Kyrell smiles at him before turning his attention to Zane. "Why weren't you at the tux fitting, bro?"

Zane hugs Kyrell. "Not all of us are billionaire playboys." He jokes. "I'm a mere mortal who has to work."

"Nah, but you could be. Are you still down for a meeting with Titan Tech? They could really use someone with your brilliance."

Titan Tech was Kyrell's dad's company. He inherited it, and billions of dollars, after his dad passed away. Elias, his dad, gave him the option to keep the company or sell it. He chose to sell it because he didn't want to try and fill his dad's shoes and he wants to create his own legacy. Even though Kyrell isn't directly involved with Titan Tech, he still has the connections. Zane is a software developer and Kyrell has been encouraging him to consider working for Titan Tech.

"Hell yeah, I am," Zane says. "We'll talk more about it later, though. I'm here to let loose."

"And this is why I married you." Sevyn kisses his cheek.

Acyn chuckles. "Shall we head to the hotel?"

"Yeah, let's do this shit." Kyrell smiles.

The guys carry our luggage out to the car while Sevyn, Quinn, and I walk arm in arm behind them.

"I'm so excited! Once Marisa's here, we'll kick this weekend off with a lingerie party." Quinn smiles.

"A lingerie party?" I whip my head to look at her. "What is that?" In my head, I'm thinking of us running around in lingerie.

"We all got something to make your honeymoon a little spicier." Quinn winks at me.

"Why do I feel like your horny ass is behind this, Sevyn?" I laugh.

"Pinterest in the middle of a sleepless night always provides one with great ideas." Sevyn flips her hair over her shoulder.

"Greyson's fiancé didn't want to come?" Quinn asks once we reach the suburban awaiting us.

"Selene wanted to come, but she couldn't get the time off work."

"Oh, that sucks. She's really nice. I'll send her all the swag," Quinn says.

"She'd love that," I say.

The driver smiles as he opens the Suburban door for us. Me and the girls pile into the back row of seats and continue our conversation about our plans. Acyn, Zane, and Kyrell are talking about hitting up the casinos tonight.

I'm only half listening as I try to take in all the glitz and glamour of the Vegas strip. It's unlike anything else, and I can't wait to see all the neon signs glow at night. There's something to do every place my eyes look. And from what Quinn told me about the hotel we're staying in, there are an abundance of things to do there as well. One thing is for sure—Vegas is for fun.

"I thought we could go for drinks first," Quinn says.

I tear my gaze from the window, glancing at her belly, and snort with laughter. "Quinn, we can skip drinks, since it won't be enjoyable for you."

"No." She holds up her hand. "I'm not killing the vibe with my pregnant ass. I'll just get something virgin and an appetizer. No big deal."

"I'll have some virgin drinks with you." I smile at her.

I'm not really a drinker, anyway. I don't mind a good wine or mixed drink, but it's not what makes or breaks an experience for me. I'd rather have a joint or an edible. At least they don't make me feel like shit afterward.

"I support both of your decisions, but I am going to be drinking like a fish." Sevyn chimes in.

I toss my head back with laughter. "And we support that decision!"

"Don't worry, Zane will take care of me, if anything. Won't you babe?" She pats him on the shoulder.

"I love you, Sev." He turns to face her. "But it's every person for themselves this weekend." We all burst out laughing while Sevyn stares at Zane with her mouth open.

"You're so loud when you're drunk. It's not like he'll be able to ignore you even if he wanted to." Acyn smirks.

"Haha... ha." Sevyn narrows her eyes at them. "Fuck you both. I'm not loud am I, Harlow?"

"Huh?" I ask, pretending not to hear her.

Her mouth hangs open. "You're agreeing with them?"

"I–oh, look!" I point at the hotel. "We're here!"

The hotel is sleek and modern. As we get out of the car, my phone vibrates with a text.

Marisa: I'm here. Getting my bags.

Harlow: We just arrived at the hotel. Can't wait to see you!

I turn to Quinn as we walk into the lobby. "Marisa is grabbing her bags, and she'll be on her way."

"Perfect." She smiles.

The hotel lobby is all black, with immense columns that have LED screens that are playing clips of abstract art on a loop. I reach in my bag for my camera as I look around in awe.

"That didn't take long." Acyn chuckles beside me.

"I know, I was trying to not take a billion pictures... but I have to."

He wraps his arm around my neck and kisses my temple. "Take a billion pictures, Sunshine."

Acyn gets it. Photography is second nature to me. People ask how I enjoy the moment if I'm always busy taking pictures. Truth is, I am enjoying the moment–savoring it–with each photo my camera captures. I look for the little things that no one else notices but will want to remember. Through my lens, I see Quinn smiling at Kyrell as he palms her belly and talks to their baby. Zane stands behind Sevyn with his arms wrapped around her shoulders and a look of contentedness on their faces. And when I focus my lens on Acyn, all I see is the love and admiration he has for me. These are the moments I capture. I get to remember them forever.

Kyrell finishes up at the reception desk and turns to us, handing me a key. "I got you and Acyn a suite so you two can bang at your leisure." He smirks.

"You're so annoying, but thank you." I laugh.

Chuckling, Acyn shrugs. "At least you know what it is."

"The rest of us will stay in two separate suites." Kyrell says. "One for the ladies and one for the gents, but we're all on the same floor to make it easier to link up."

"We're doing our own thing tonight, right?" I ask.

"Harls, you know I never have a plan. I just go with what feels right." Kyrell winks.

"Yes, we're doing our own thing." Quinn chimes in. The calm to Kyrell's chaos. "We'll meet up for breakfast and some shows, but the night is our own. I figured we could get ready, have the lingerie party, and then go get drinks."

"Lingerie party?" all three men ask in unison.

We stare back at them. "You wouldn't get it." I smile at Acyn and continue talking to the girls. "Okay, I guess we'll all get situated. What time should we plan to meet up?"

Quinn glances at her watch. "Meet us in our suite in an hour for the party, and then we can go for drinks from there."

"Perfect."

"They already took your bags up to the room. I guess we'll meet in an hour, too," Kyrell says to Acyn.

We all pile into the elevator, and I send Marisa a text with the room number.

Marisa: Okay, Grey and Ash are with me too.

Harlow: See you in a bit!

We go our separate ways once we get to our floor. Acyn and I enter our suite, which is more like an apartment. Light is spilling into the room from the floor to ceiling windows. The walls are decorated with vibrant art. It's spacious, with a living and dining room that has a wet bar. It's nearly as big as the guest house I stayed in when I first moved to Seattle. I open one of the sliding doors that leads out to the wrap around terrace. The view is gorgeous.

"This place is unbelievable." Acyn wraps his arms around my waist. "I can't wait to see all the lights at night from up here."

"Are you happy we chose Vegas now?"

"Yes!" I turn around and kiss him. "Very happy."

My phone vibrates in my back pocket. I pull it out and look at the two texts.

Marisa: Hurry up and get ready!

Quinn: Don't forget we're meeting in an hour.

They know me too well. "The girls will have my head if I'm not knocking on their door in approximately one hour." I kiss him again. "I have to get ready."

"You know..." he kisses my neck. "We are in the desert. May as well conserve water and shower together."

"The exhibitionist turned environmentalist. I gladly support both of your causes."

He picks me up, causing me to shriek with laughter as I wrap my legs around his middle.

"I could fuck you on the balcony too, but I take it you want to be on time?" He carries me into the bathroom.

"I feel you're the higher priority right now." I pull my shirt overhead, tossing it on the bathroom floor.

He unsnaps my bra and trails kisses across my breasts before setting me down so I can take off my jeans. My lips meet his as he steps out of his own. He picks me up again before stepping into the shower and turning on the water without his lips leaving mine. Once steam billows around us, he presses me up against the glass shower door. I reach down between us, grabbing his length, and guide him inside me. My breath hitches as he buries himself. He presses one hand against the shower door and his other hand grips my ass as I keep my legs and arms tightly wrapped around him. A moan spills from my lips as he sucks on one nipple before taking the other into his mouth as he thrusts into me.

He trails kisses up my neck before meeting my lips again. "Turn around for me," he mumbles against my lips.

I untangle myself from him, turning around, and press my palms against the shower wall. Slightly bending forward, he grips my hip and pushes into my wetness. As he thrusts into me, I let out a moan that reverberates off the shower walls. He grips my hair, pulling me back flush against his chest, and his other hand plays with my clit. I spread my legs further apart and feel my climax building. The tingle starts in my toes as my body grows hot as he thrusts into me. He kisses my neck before gently grazing my skin with his teeth.

My body never knows what to do when Acyn touches me. I go into overdrive and short circuit at the same time. It's pleasure overload as he massages my center, grips my hair, kisses my neck, and fucks me at the same damn time. I quickly dissolve into pleasure as my orgasm shudders through me. I moan loudly while calling out his name. Acyn pounds into me as he chases his release.

He finds it moments later as his body tenses and quakes as he spills into me. I rest my head against the shower wall, trying to catch my breath. Acyn slowly pulls out of me and turns me around to face him. He kisses me softly.

"I'm addicted to the feel of you."

"What gave it away?" I wrap my arms around his neck. "The fact we're married or that we can't keep our hands off of each other?"

"Both." He chuckles, giving me another kiss before stepping underneath the rain shower faucet above our heads.

I watch the water soak his curls, making them longer, so they hang a little past his brows. My eyes follow the water as it flows over his closed eyes, soft lips, abs, and–

"Sunshine, if you don't get ready, you're gonna be late." His eyes are on me again with a smirk on his lips.

"Why did you interrupt my ogling?" I continue lathering my body with soap.

"Ogle away, but I know your friends and they'll kidnap you if they have to."

A little while later, I'm putting on my earrings as I look at myself in the mirror. I love the way my gold sequined mini skirt catches the light whenever I move. It makes my deep golden brown skin glow. I paired it with a white blouse that plunges low and loosely criss crosses in the front. Placing my hand on the wall, I steady myself as I slide on my ankle strap Christian Louboutin heels. I straighten up, fixing my curls as I turn side to side in the mirror.

"Sunshine, have you seen–" He stops in his tracks, and his eyes rake over my body. "You look incredible."

"Thank you." I smile. "You do too."

Acyn is wearing a black satin button up that has a muted shine with the top buttons undone, and it's tucked into his slim fitting black pants. It's clear he rarely misses a morning run or the gym. He's paired it with a black Fendi belt and loafers that have gold accents.

"Did you need something?"

"Oh." He tears his eyes away from my legs. "Did you pack my jewelry?"

"Yep, it's in my suitcase." His eyes are already back on my legs again. I bend forward, pretending to fix the strap around my ankle, and then slowly trail my hand up my leg.

"Those legs of yours. I look forward to them being draped over my shoulders with those heels by my ears later."

"That was a detailed description." I smirk. "I'll be sure to leave them on for you. For now, I have to meet the girls before they come for me."

He chuckles. "Alright."

"Love you. I'll see you when I see you because only heaven knows what you guys will get into with Kyrell. Enjoy your night."

"Have fun with the girls. Love you too, Sunshine." He kisses me again before I walk out the door.

CHAPTER 11

Harlow

Marisa wraps me in a neck breaking hug as soon as I step into their suite. I wrap my arms around her as I try to laugh.

"You're crushing my windpipe," I choke out.

"Sorry, sorry!" She loosens her arms from around my neck but doesn't let go. "I just missed you."

"Missed you too, babe."

"Is she trying to murder you, too?" Quinn asks as she enters the room.

"Yes." I snort with laughter. "Tell Acyn I love him."

Marisa finally releases me. "You two are so fucking dramatic." She rolls her eyes.

I rub my neck. "I feel our reaction is warranted."

Marisa looks different. Her curly black hair, that was once down to her waist, is now shoulder length.

"Your hair looks amazing! When did you cut it? I only saw you a week ago and you now look like a brand new woman."

We religiously video chat every weekend. With us all living in different places, it's the only way we can keep up with each other.

"I said the same thing." Quinn laughs.

Marisa fluffs up her curls. "Do you really think it looks good?"

She's had waist length hair since we met three years ago. Marisa is gorgeous with her deep brown skin, large hazel eyes, full lips, and toned curvy body from all the yoga she does. She could have the worst haircut and would still be beautiful.

"Yes! Do you not like it?"

"It's just taking some getting used to. It was a rash decision." Her eyes meet the floor.

"Did something happen?" I gently touch her arm.

Sevyn enters the room with a mixed drink in hand. She runs her fingers through Marisa's hair. "You're crazy to think it doesn't look good."

Quinn echoes my question. "Did something happen?"

Marisa smiles. "I'll tell you guys another time." She waves her hand. "We're here to celebrate and have fun. What are we doing first?"

I study her for a moment, wondering what happened that she's not telling us. She keeps smiling at me, and I decide to let it go. She'll talk about it when and if she wants to.

"The lingerie party!" Quinn says, clapping her hands together with a smile.

I look around their suite for the first time to realize it's decorated. There's a wall for taking pictures covered in lush greenery and sunflowers with gold letters hanging that say, "Miss to Mrs". It's surrounded by gold and white balloons. As I slowly turn around the room, I realize there are actually balloons and streamers everywhere I look. There's a table covered in beautifully wrapped presents and a table with various drinks, a charcuterie board, and a small gold platter with edibles.

"This is amazing, you guys. I love it." I beam at them.

"To be fair, Quinn did all the planning." Marisa says. "And all the decorating. We just gave a little input here and there."

"Oh, please!" Quinn waves her hand. "It was a group effort."

"Thank you." I smile at Quinn. She's the planner out of the four of us and clearly has an eye for design.

"Are we going to get this party started or what?" Sevyn asks. "I'm trying to get as many drinks into my system as possible."

"That's the spirit!" Marisa gives her a high-five.

"And this is why I'm not drinking. I can't leave Quinn to take care of all of us." I say.

"You're not drinking at your own bachelorette party?" Marisa gives me an incredulous look.

"Do y'all not remember the engagement party? The bad karaoke and then slipping off the stage. Acyn literally had to carry me out to the car, and I puked all over the seats—" They all laugh hysterically at the memory. "—And him. It was a fucking mess." I laugh. "Drinking is fun until you're puking everywhere. I'm fine with a couple of cute mixed drinks and an edible."

"Oh my God!" Sevyn wheezes. "I'm surprised you even remember that."

"I didn't. Kyrell showed me the video. I was so fucking embarrassed. Never again." I cover my face.

"It was your engagement party! You had every right to have a good time!" Marisa says through laughter.

"I'd rather not talk about this. Can we start the party?" I ask, desperate to change the subject.

"Okay, first up! We have something specially made for us by Sevyn." Quinn says, handing me a bag.

It's yellow with gold tissue paper sticking out of the top. Pulling out the paper, I reach into the bag and pull out a soft, white satin robe. When I unfold it, I read 'Mrs. DeConto' embroidered in black cursive on the back.

"Oh my God!" I squeal. "Sev, this is amazing." I get up and hug her. "Thank you."

"You're welcome." She hugs me back. "I wanted to do something different, so I thought why not Mrs. DeConto instead of the basic ass 'bride' on the back?"

"I love it so much!" I exclaim, hugging it to my body.

"She made some for us too, with our names on the back." Marisa grabs a bag off the table and pulls hers out.

"Babes... you know this means we have to take a picture, right?"

They laugh, already knowing what it is, as they pull out their robes and slip them on. We take countless pictures of us in front of the photo backdrop. Once I'm satisfied with the pictures, I take an edible, and they pass me the gifts on the table.

"There are some from everyone, including Gloria and Ava." Quinn says.

My eyes widen. "What? You told them to get me lingerie?"

Sevyn cackles. "You act like they haven't had sex before, Harlow."

"I know... but it's awkward."

Marisa sucks her teeth. "Girl, please! Free shit? Open it."

She has a point. Lingerie isn't cheap. For the next thirty minutes, I tear through gift after gift filled with the most beautifully designed, intricate lingerie I've ever seen in my life. Gloria gave me a gorgeous red silk slip dress with scalloped lace and foiled embroidery. Ava gave me a violet silk teddy that has ruffles around the thighs. I also received gifts from my assistant, Priscilla, and my former boss, Celeste. Aside from lingerie, each of the girls gave me a toy as well. Sevyn got me a vibrator, Marisa some divine smelling massage oils and black leather cuffs with a buckle closure, and Quinn gave me THC and CBD infused lube with a pretty rose quartz dildo. I'm looking forward to wearing and using all of this with Acyn.

"I'm low-key jealous Acyn gets to see you in all of this and not us," Marisa says.

"I know!" Sevyn whines. "I was trying to get her to tell me the dirty details of the post-wedding sex, but she was being a prude."

I cackle. "Sevyn! He's your brother, for fuck's sake!"

"It's not a secret, though. From the way you've stayed glowing since getting with him, we know the dick is sending you to other dimensions." Quinn side eyes me with a smirk.

I look at her belly. "You're one to talk."

"The dick was so good Quinn got knocked up." Sevyn cackles. "Been there. Done that. Have the kids to fucking prove it!"

"I'm going to tell our kid a beautiful love story that is worthy of being a book, okay?" Quinn says. "Not that Daddy was putting it down and Mommy couldn't get enough." We fall into a fit of laughter.

"Okay, okay!" Marisa says once she catches her breath. She grabs the bottle of tequila off the table and three shot glasses. "Do at least one shot with us."

"Yeah, you know your limits after the engagement party. A few couldn't hurt." Sevyn encourages me.

"Harls, this is your bachelorette party. Enjoy yourself." Quinn nudges my arm.

"I never said no to drinks. I said no to getting blitzed." I hold my hand out for a shot glass.

"I'd like to make a toast to Harlow choosing the same dick for the rest of her life." Marisa raises her glass into the air.

I snort with laughter. "I will gladly get on all fours, face down, ass up, for the rest of my life for Acyn!"

Quinn has her phone out recording and laughing while the three of us throw the shots back.

"One more," I say, and Marisa gladly pours us another round. I toss that one back too. "Okay, third times a charm, right?" I wipe my mouth with the back of my hand.

"Aye, that a girl!" Sevyn says, pouring herself a fourth shot.

"I need food in my system before these drinks and edible go straight to my head."

Quinn glances down at her watch. "Let's go get some food. The other two can get drinks and we can eat."

"I need food too. And more drinks." Sevyn smiles.

We stumble out into the hallway, talking and laughing. I met Quinn and Marisa when I didn't know who I was and met Sevyn when I was trying to find myself. Since it was only my dad and me, female support was something I was lacking and didn't really know. But now I have a group of amazing and endlessly supportive women in my life. I'd be lost without them.

The next morning, Acyn and I are the last to join everyone for breakfast. It's apparent it was our first night in Vegas because everyone but Quinn looks severely hungover. Kyrell is a seasoned partier and is guzzling water with a bottle of Tylenol next to him. Zane has his arm wrapped around Sevyn, who is resting her head on his shoulder with her eyes closed, as he drinks his coffee. Marisa has shades on with an oversized sunhat. She looks regal for being hungover. Asher is having a mixed drink with his breakfast and Greyson looks like he's still half asleep.

We take our seats next to Quinn and Kyrell. I lean against Acyn and let out a yawn, pulling my sunglasses down over my eyes.

"You good, Sunshine?" he asks, smirking at me.

"It'd be great if we'd stop moving."

He chuckles. "What happened to no drinks?"

"I wish I knew," I groan.

Last night I lost track of my drinks. We had an amazing time, eating, walking the strip, going into Casinos, and we ended the night dancing. Quinn texted Kyrell to let him know where we were, and the guys met up with us. When I looked at my camera reel, I had to laugh because the pictures progressively got blurrier. I wasn't engagement party shitfaced, but I was definitely flirting with that line again.

"Here. Eat something." He holds a strawberry up to my face from one of the many breakfast platters on the table. I open my mouth for him to feed me.

Food has no appeal right now, but I know I need it because it'll help me feel better.

"God, I love the way he cares for you," Marisa says with her chin resting in her hand as she looks at us.

I kiss Acyn. "You take the best care of me."

"Of course, I do. Cause I love you." He feeds me another bite of food.

"You're still single Marisa?" Asher asks from the other end of the table.

"Don't remind me." She sighs, leaning back into her seat.

"Being single isn't that bad," he says, taking a bite of pancake.

"Eh... it is when all your friends are in relationships. I'm in no rush, but I also want a man to dote on me."

"Preach, babygirl! Preach!" Sevyn says, waving her napkin in the air.

"If you're down, I'm down Marisa. The last two standing. May as well give it a shot." He leans forward, resting his forearms on the table.

"Thanks, Ash." She flips her hair over her shoulder. "But I don't need nor want a pity fuck."

We all laugh, even Asher. I think he may actually like her for real, though. They always pair up whenever we get together, but nothing has happened between them other than banter and flirting.

"You know where to find me if you ever change your mind." He winks.

Marisa stares at him a moment, considering his words, before turning her attention back to me.

"Ready for round two?" she asks.

I raise up my hands. "Hell no. Fuck that. You and Sevyn can keep it. I'll be joining Quinn on the sidelines."

"Had enough fun already, Harls?" Quinn asks, chuckling beside me.

"No, not enough fun. Enough drinking." I adjust my sunglasses, resting my head against Acyn's shoulder again. He hands me a glass of water that I drink in a few gulps. I'm slowly feeling better. "What's on the agenda for today?"

"Zip lining," Kyrell says.

"Are you serious?" I sit up and look at him with a smile on my face.

"Yep. We're supposed to be there at 1:00 this afternoon if everyone can get their asses in gear."

"I'm considering sitting this one out," Greyson says. "I'd be doing a public service because I'll probably puke on someone's head."

"I feel your pain, Grey," Zane says with a nod.

"Oh, please!" Sevyn says, sucking her teeth. "Men are so whiney. It's a hangover. Take some Tylenol, eat some food, and keep the party moving."

"Tell 'em, sis!" Marisa claps her hands while laughing.

"I didn't complain. I'm zip lining," Asher says. "Puke or not. It's their fault for walking underneath me."

"Your level of arrogance is—" Marisa starts.

"Sexy?" Asher flashes her a smile.

She narrows her eyes. "Unbelievable was the word on the tip of my tongue before you so arrogantly interrupted me. I have yet to see sexy coming from you."

I really need them to figure out what it is they have going on. They fight like this every time we're together. It has to be sexual tension because they both seem to enjoy it a little too much.

I grab Acyn's wrist to check the time. "Oh good, I can take a nap."

"You'll definitely need your rest." Sevyn wags her eyebrows. "We've got a Thunder from Down Under show tonight. Don't want you to miss all those oily, ripped bodies."

Acyn coughs as he takes a sip of orange juice.

"Are you okay?" I side eye him with a smirk.

"Yeah, I just—what time is this at?"

"Plot twist. I'm not the jealous one." I laugh. "No one has anything on your stripper moves, babe."

"Stripper moves?" Kyrell asks with a raised eyebrow.

"He stripped for me in front of our neighbors." Acyn tosses his head back with laughter.

"Dance stripped or took off his clothes stripped?" Marisa asks.

"Both!" I snort with laughter.

"She said she wanted a stripper." Acyn shrugs. "So I gave her a stripper."

"Was he any good?" Quinn tries to bite back a smile.

"Yeah, was he?" Marisa asks fanning herself with a napkin.

"Shit, I'm curious too," Kyrell adds and laughter ripples around the table.

"If I had cash on me, it would've been raining!" I swipe my hand across the other as if I'm throwing money.

"Ace, maybe you have a career in the performing arts." Zane says.

"I'm a man of many talents." Acyn grins.

We recap our night, laughing at each other for the dumb shit we did. Thankfully, none of us did anything too wild, but tonight is when our actual parties will be. After zip lining, I'm going to hang out with the girls for the rest of the day so they can help me get ready. It's been fun to spend time with the guys, but still do our own thing.

"Alright, I have to go prepare myself for a day of fuckery." Asher finishes his drink and slides his chair back as he stands.

"I should probably get ready too." Marisa takes her last bite of food and waves before heading back inside.

"Let's all meet in the lobby at 12:30. Sound good?" Quinn asks.

We all nod or say yes. Acyn and I sit at the table chatting with Greyson, Quinn, Kyrell, Sevyn, and Zane a little longer. By the end of breakfast, I feel much better.

"Are you ready to go, Sunshine?" Acyn asks, stretching in his seat and yawning.

"Yeah. We'll see you guys soon." I say to everyone still at the table.

As we head up to our room, I hop on Acyn's back. He grabs my thighs; I wrap my arms around his shoulders and kiss his neck. Once we're in the elevator, he sets me down and presses me against the wall before his lips meet mine. There's something about elevators. He wraps his arm around my waist, pulling me flush against him. His other hand roams over my body while my hands slip under his shirt to feel on his abs. I let out a moan when he dips his hand into the front of my sweats and applies pressure to my clit. He rubs in slow circles, and I let my head fall back as the pleasure washes over me. I have to admit, there's something thrilling about the possibility of getting caught. But in the heat of the moment, it's the furthest thing from my mind. I don't feel the elevator slow or hear the ding of the doors, but I hear the gasps.

I pull away from Acyn to see a group of women staring at us with their mouths open. Acyn's hand is still down my pants, and I'm not sure what to do. They already know what we're doing. We were so caught up in the moment that we didn't pull away. But now I'm trying to push Acyn off me, slightly mortified, but he refuses to move.

"Uh..." the woman says, blinking rapidly. "We can catch the next one and let you two... uh... finish." She smiles as she backs up.

"You do that," Acyn says, tapping the button for the doors to close, and his lips are on mine before I can utter a word.

I push against his chest, and he reluctantly pulls away from me. "Something wrong, Sunshine?" he asks, resting his forehead against mine.

"You're really going to pretend a group of women didn't just see you with your hand down my pants?" I ask, biting back a laugh.

It quickly turns into a whimper as he massages my clit again. "I know, but don't give a fuck. Now, we have about a minute before we reach our floor with the possibility of more stops. Let me make you cum." He dips his finger inside me before rubbing it over my clit again.

I can't give a verbal response as my body hums with pleasure. Instead, I lift my leg up to give him easier access and he grips my thigh as he rubs my clit while kissing my neck and makes me cum in the elevator.

CHAPTER 12

Harlow's Bachelorette Party

Zip lining was a blast, even though Quinn couldn't go with us because of her baby bump. She was on the verge of tears when she realized she couldn't join. Kyrell promised her another trip to Vegas once the baby's here. I couldn't blame her because it was a fun experience, but I also told her she wouldn't have to babysit tonight because I'd be sober. That seemed to lift her spirits a little.

After we're done zip lining, we go our separate ways.

"Don't run away with some Aussie, alright?" Acyn kisses my neck.

I snort with laughter. "Damn, that's been my plan this whole time."

He gives me a kiss that Sevyn interrupts.

"Alright, yeah! You've had enough of her. Save some for the rest of us." She pulls me away from him. "I'll make sure she only gets a lap dance, bro," she says over her shoulder as she escorts me to the car.

I toss my head back with laughter. "You're so comforting."

"You're telling me you don't wanna be tossed around like a rag doll by some ripped guy?"

"Uh... well, your brother already does that daily."

Sevyn gasps. "I fucking knew it!"

"Knew what?" Quinn and Marisa ask when we slide into our seats.

"That Acyn tosses her around during sex," Sevyn says loudly, and the driver tries to keep his eyes on the road but is now looking at Sev in the rearview mirror.

They both laugh. "How are you just now finding out Harlow is a freak?" Quinn asks.

"She won't tell me anything because he's my brother!"

"It doesn't bother you?" Marisa asks.

"I literally saw him eating her out against my garage door—" Quinn and Marisa gasp "—it doesn't bother me."

"Wait, what?" Quinn sits up a little straighter and leans forward to look at me.

"Yeah, when the fuck did this happen?" Marisa tilts her head to the side.

"Sevyn!" I groan. "You weren't supposed to say anything about that."

"I feel betrayed right now," Quinn says dramatically. "Keeping dirty little secrets from us."

"It's not even like that. I just..." My voice trails off.

"Then what was it like?" Marisa raises a brow.

Sevyn is sitting with her arms folded and a smug smile on her lips, waiting for me to tell them.

I let out an exasperated sigh. "It was when we got together. We hadn't been talking for two weeks and then he kissed me..."

"Okay, but how did his lips end up between your legs against Sevyn's garage door?" Quinn asks.

"Heat of the moment..." I shrug. "He got on his knees in front of me and—"

"Wait, he got on his knees in front of you?" Marisa's mouth hangs open. "That is the sexiest shit I've ever heard in my fucking life."

"Exactly! How was I supposed to tell him to stop? So, he just... ripped my panties off and ate me for lunch. Then Sevyn caught us."

"Ripped your panties off?" Quinn fans herself.

"Oh my God! You guys act like you don't have amazing sex." Heat creeps up my neck.

"Always the quiet ones, I tell you." Sevyn points at me.

I swat at her, laughing. "Shut up!"

"I'm definitely not having sex like that," Marisa scoffs. "I mean, it gets the job done, but they aren't worshipping me. This is when I hate being single."

"I'm sure Asher would love to change that for you." I smirk and look out the window. "We're not going back to the hotel?"

Quinn shakes her head. "Nope. We're going to the spa first, then we'll head back to get ready. I thought some pampering couldn't hurt."

The driver pulls up in front of an extravagant building and opens the car door for us. Walking into the spa makes me feel like I'm in Morocco, with the intricate design and décor. The aromatic scent of Palo Santo wafts around us. We have a reservation, but choose two services each so that we're all done around the same time. I choose a HydraFacial and a full body hot stone massage. Once we've chosen what we want, we're escorted to a dressing room where we change into plush white robes. I ask one of the spa staff to take a picture of us doing our best model poses. They take a few before inviting us back to begin our massages.

I slip out of my robe and lie face down on the massage table. When I was teaching yoga I would get regular massages, but then I focused more on my photography career and can't remember the last time I got one. As soon as the massage therapist's hands touch my back, I melt into the table. I can't help the moan that comes out of my mouth.

"Whatever massage you're having, I want it," Sevyn says.

"Shut up, Sevyn." I chuckle. "Quinn, I can tell you this is by far better than zip lining."

"I'm in heaven," Quinn mumbles.

"We're right there with you, babe," Marisa adds.

Talking subsides as we enjoy our massages. After a long night of drinking and dancing, this is exactly what I need. Sooner than I'd like, we're heading for our facials. To my surprise, the facial is just as relaxing as the massage. I've never had one before, but as I look at my dewy, supple skin in the mirror, I'll make it a regular thing. It's amazing how I'm glowing. Now that we're polished and radiant, we're ready to have fun with the men at the strip show.

Marisa applies lashes after doing my eyeshadow and eyeliner. I've never worn false lashes before and am anxious to see what they look like.

"I'm almost done," she mumbles distractedly. Moments later, she holds a mirror up to my face.

I gasp. "That's me?"

"Yes. Do you like them? I tried to keep them minimal, but just enough to make your lashes look fuller."

"I fucking love them!" I look at myself from every angle. "Can you come do my lashes for me all the time?"

"I wish I lived a little closer, then I totally would."

She lives a few hours away in Portland. She's close, but not close enough.

"I think a red lip would look fire on you with your leather and lace get up. Fuck around and really go home with an Aussie."

"Accents are nice," I smirk.

"A true weakness of mine." She gently grabs my face to apply the lipstick.

Since we're alone in the room, I decide to ask her about the haircut. "What happened with the hair?"

Her hand freezes. "It's a long story... and I don't want to dampen the mood."

"Where are we hiding the body?"

She laughs as she sits next to me on the bed. "Remember the guy I was telling you guys about that I met a few months ago at the bar?"

I nod my head. "You guys hit it off, right?"

"He was perfect. Handsome, charming... an actual dream, you know?"

I think of Acyn. Although I wouldn't have initially said he was charming. "What happened?"

"He was married... with kids. This whole fucking life."

"Did you know this or?" I search her face.

"No, I didn't know. I didn't have a fucking clue. Harls, he had an apartment and everything. I thought he was who he told me he was the first night we met." Her eyes well with tears, and I place my hand on her back.

"H-How did you find out?"

She hesitates, and we sit in silence for a moment. "His wife... I found out from his wife."

"Wait..." I sit up a little straighter. "What? How?"

"God, it was a fucking mess." She sighs and looks down at her hands. "She signed up for private lessons at my studio. She came in twice a week, and we hit it off. Even went to coffee and brunch together a few times. She told me all about her family and her husband. Then, after a couple of months of this, she invited me over to her house... *their* house for a dinner party."

I don't like where this is going, but I keep my mouth shut because I want to hear the full story. She continues. "I get to the dinner party and there are quite a few people there. And not just random people, but people who are prominent in Portland. People who can help you make a name for yourself. I was honored to be in such a space." She smiles briefly, and it fades.

"But then... he walked in. He didn't see me at first, but I saw him walk toward the woman I considered a friend and kiss her on the lips. And I felt... gutted. Everything I thought I knew was a fucking lie. The man who I let into my life, my heart, my bed... I let him into everything and there he was with his wife. It felt like a double-edged sword because I actually considered her a friend, too."

I hold her hand because I don't know what else to do as I listen to her tell me about this lying piece of shit. She inhales deeply. "She brought him over to me, and he knew he was fucked when his eyes landed on mine. All I could do was stand there frozen, staring at him, wondering what the fuck I'd done. As if things couldn't get worse, his wife made a toast introducing me as his 'whore mistress.'"

I gasp, covering my mouth. "That bitch did not! What about her cheating, lying ass husband who can't keep his dick in his pants?"

"My thoughts exactly." She laughs. "After she did that, I sort of snapped out of it and told her maybe if she was more of a whore like me, he wouldn't be in my bed at night. Needless to say, I got a glass of wine thrown in my face, but it was fucking worth it."

I fall back onto the bed with laughter. "Marisa! You did not!"

"I sure as hell did. Fuck that bitch and her man, too." She laughs. "But..." she sighs, falling back onto the bed next to me. "I fucking loved him, Harls. I still do. And I hate that about myself. I feel ridiculous for falling for a man who only saw me as a novelty. It fucking hurts and I'm lonely. So... as any woman does who wants to change her life and the world after heartbreak, she cuts her hair."

I give her a small smile. "I'm sorry that happened to you. Marisa, you're gorgeous inside and out. None of this is your fault. There is no way you could've known that he was lying sack of shit. Fuck him and his wife, just like you said."

"I love you, Harlow." She hugs me, kissing my cheek.

"I love you too, babe."

Quinn peeks her head into the room before stepping inside. "Oh." She puts her hands on her hips. "You two thought you could have a romance without me?"

"I'm always down for a ménage à trois," Marisa says, holding her arm out.

"What are we talking about?" Quinn wedges herself between us. "Are you okay?" she asks Marisa.

"I am now, but I'll tell you another time." Marisa smiles at her. "I've gotta finish getting our Queen ready."

Marisa finishes my hair and makeup; now it's time for the outfit. I put on a black lace bustier top that gives the illusion my breasts are a split second away from spilling out. Then I pull on my black leather miniskirt that has a high slit on the front of the left thigh. I slide a glittery gold thigh chain on for a little extra detail.

"Can you guys see my ass cheeks if I bend over?" I bend forward slightly.

"Yes, but the skirt is cute. Wear it. It's Vegas, baby! Be a showgirl!" Sevyn shouts.

"That thigh chain in sexy as hell," Quinn says.

"Ow, ow, ow! Legs for fucking days!" Marisa whistles. "Put the heels on. I'm trying to get the full Harlow experience right now."

I giggle as they hype me up and put on my heels. They have a gold ankle strap with a gold heel, and black soles. I stand in front of the mirror, feeling like a total bombshell.

"Ugh, I'm feelin' myself y'all!" I run my hands over my body.

"That leather and lace is working for you, babe!" Marisa says. "You're gonna break necks."

"We all are." I turn around to look at them. "We came to slay, not to play tonight."

Marisa is wearing a high waisted mini skirt with a belt cinched at her waist, and a sheer body suit with embroidery detail that covers her nipples. She paired it with some strappy black heels. Quinn adjusts her baby pink slip dress with a scoop neckline and two high slits on the side that she paired with thigh high heels. Whenever I get pregnant, I hope to be as fashionable as she is. Sevyn is wearing red leather pants with a white bodysuit that has a plunging neckline, almost to her navel, and no back with black sky high heels. We are all definitely going to get some attention tonight, and I love that for us.

After a round of pictures, I immediately upload them to Instagram, and then we head out for our show. There's nothing like a little glam and your besties hyping you up for a boost of confidence. We're talking and laughing as we spill into the lobby from the elevator. I reach into my clutch for my phone when I bump into a hard chest.

"Oh, excuse me. I—"

"Look fucking incredible. God fucking damn," a deep voice that calls to my soul says.

I look into Acyn's eyes, and they're ablaze for me. "Thank you." I simper.

"No. Thank you for being my wife."

"Forever a pleasure." I smile at him before glancing at his entourage and realize we stopped them in their tracks. Mission accomplished.

Acyn turns to Kyrell, who's currently feeling up Quinn. "Do we really have to go out tonight?" His heated gaze is on me again.

"I was wondering the same shit, bro." He kisses Quinn's neck as she giggles.

"Well, this makes me feel like a lonely fucker without Selene here." Greyson says, looking at all of us. Acyn's about to respond when Sevyn raises her voice.

"Back up!" Sevyn smooshes Zane's face with her hand. "I have no time for this. We have a date with some male strippers. You can have your way with me after."

Marisa cackles. "He just wants to appreciate you looking like his last meal."

"Yeah, Sevyn. Let me show you my appreciation." Zane continues to feel her up.

"That's too damn bad! I've been looking forward to this all day. I am going to see sweaty, ripped men, and then I will come back and fuck my husband." Sevyn grabs my hand, trying to pull me in the opposite direction.

"Marisa, I can show you some appreciation right now," Asher cuts in.

"What is with you horn dogs?" Sevyn asks, exasperated.

"You're really one to talk, Sev," I snort with laughter.

Marisa gives Asher an appraising look. "We'll see if I go home with a dancer or not. I'll let you know." She smirks.

Acyn grips my ass and smacks it before kissing me. "I can't wait to taste you and hear you scream my name later," he whispers in my ear.

"You should probably know I don't have any panties on," I whisper back before Sevyn, Marisa, and Quinn pull me in the opposite direction.

I peek over my shoulder at him before we walk out the door, and I feel the pulse between my thighs at the look of desire in his eyes.

We arrive a little early for the show and they give us a round of jello shots. Despite saying I wouldn't drink tonight, the girls encourage me to take a shot.

"I refuse to rain on anyone's parade," says Quinn with a smile as I grab a shot.

I squeeze my eyes shut as it slides down my throat. "I won't get sauced. I promise."

I'm excited, but I had to take an edible to calm my nerves because I don't know what to expect at this show. I've never been to a strip club before, and I want to enjoy myself. Marisa and Sevyn down the rest of the shots. When they're done with them, they pop open a bottle of champagne.

"We're gonna have to carry them back, aren't we?" I ask Quinn as we watch them down glasses of champagne.

"It's only a matter of time before they pass out."

I giggle as the lights dim. A mixture of excitement and nervousness come over me. I could barely handle Acyn dancing on me, let alone watching professional dancers.

"Yes! Show us the dick!" Marisa shouts.

I slap my hand over my mouth, laughing hysterically. "Are we going to actually see dick?"

"I've heard these shows can get pretty wild." Quinn shrugs with a mischievous glint in her eye. "I guess we'll have to see."

The dancers come out on stage and the crowd goes wild. It's hard to tell what they look like because it's dark and their heads are down. I can tell they all spend hours in the gym, though. Music cuts through the cheering. When the beat drops, they look up in unison and begin their performance. Despite their size, they move around the stage effortlessly in sync. Marisa nearly drops her glass of champagne when they rip off their shirts. Quinn tosses her head back with laughter, and I can't help but giggle, too. I settle into my seat as the performance continues, realizing this isn't anything like I was expecting. They turn their backs to the crowd as the music stops and rip off their pants to reveal bright blue breifs. We gasp. I feel I should look away, but I can't, and the row of men flash their asses at the audience. The screams and cheers go up a notch. They pull their briefs up before facing the front of the stage again and thrust their hips so their packages bounce around.

I spoke too soon. *This* is what I expected. I've never been around this many dicks at one time in my life. Maybe another shot earlier wouldn't have hurt. I'm by no means a prude, but I truly don't know what to do with this many nearly naked oiled men dancing in front of me. Apparently, neither does Quinn as she stares at them with her mouth open. Marisa is definitely in her element, and Sevyn is downing another glass of champagne as she looks at them over the rim. Before I can take it all in, the men jump off the stage and come into the crowd. I feel the heat creep up my neck, and my face grows hot as one of them beelines for where we're sitting. All I can hope is he doesn't come for me.

But he does. Marisa, Quinn, and Sevyn cheer him on as he takes my hand and places it on his chest. My heart stutters in my own.

He leans down and asks, "Wanna come up on stage?"

I glance at the girls, realizing this is all a fucking setup. They think I won't go up there as they laugh at me. Well, the jokes on them. It's my bachelorette party, after all.

I turn my attention back to the man in front of me and say, "Yes."

He gives me a megawatt smile and holds out his hand.

"Atta girl!" Quinn yells.

I'm not sure what I'm getting into, but I soon find out as he flips me over his shoulder and carries me to the stage. For the first time in my life, I regret not wearing panties. I hold on to my skirt in hopes it's dark enough that no one gets a free show from me. My hand slips on his oiled back as I try to hold myself up, so I don't face plant into his ass.

He sits me on a chair that's center stage, and my heart races. I try to situate myself after being flipped around like a rag doll, and when I focus on his face, he still has a smile.

"Relax and enjoy yourself." He winks.

The crowd is cheering wildly, and the lights are brighter here on stage. But I forget about that once he grinds his ass in my lap. I clamp my knees together, and I don't know what the fuck to do with my sweaty hands other than keep them glued to the sides of the chair. When I steal a glance around his gyrating hips, I see the other dancers entertaining the crowd. I'm grateful all the attention isn't entirely on me, but I'm still torn between embarrassment and being impressed by how agile he is. I can appreciate his art... right?

He does a handstand in front of me, spreading his legs nearly into a full split, and slowly drops his ass back into my lap. I hear the girls over the crowd whistling and calling my name. I cover my face with my hands and can't help the laugh that escapes me. He continues to dance on my lap and around me, perfectly in sync with the rhythm of the music. Just when I think I can't take much more, the music fades into a new song. He picks me up as though I weigh nothing, carries me back to my seat, and sits me gently in it. Before he turns to leave, he kisses the top of my hand like a gentleman, as if he wasn't just humping in my face and grinding in my lap.

"You lucky bitch!" Marisa shouts over the music. "I didn't think you'd do it and lost $100 because of you!"

"You had bets?" I toss my head back with laughter.

"Of course! I was the only one who said you'd do it because you'd want to prove a point." Quinn laughs as she collects her $200 winnings from them.

"I thought you'd say no, and I would've gladly offered myself up." Marisa pours herself another glass of champagne.

"What did he feel like?" Sevyn asks. "The way he was grinding on you like he wanted to fuck you, I know you felt something."

"He's a stripper, Sev." I cackle. "He's supposed to grind on me. And to be honest... I was more worried about flashing my goodies to the audience in this short ass skirt. Warn a girl next time!"

"You look drop dead gorgeous," Quinn says. "A little peek of the kitty is a small price to pay. Now, don't play with us. What did he feel like?"

"He felt... rock hard. In more ways than one."

They gasp before we fall into a fit of laughter. You'd think none of us have been around men before the way we're acting.

"I want in on some of this action." Marisa downs her glass of champagne and adjusts her breasts. She stands and gets the attention of the dancer closest to us.

"Make us fucking proud!" Sevyn shouts, two sheets to the wind.

Marisa gladly gets picked up by him, and he carries her on stage. It's safe to say she's the wild card of our group. We're all free spirited in our own right, but she truly is on another level. Marisa is the woman they want on stage. I looked like a deer in headlights. She is eating it up and more than willing as the dancer practically fucks her on stage. I'm glad my dancer was somewhat of a gentleman. This guy clearly loves Marisa's energy. We cheer her on as she has her moment on stage.

"She's in her element!" I say to them, my voice hoarse from yelling.

"She read the assignment, that's for—" Quinn begins but stops abruptly.

"Oh, honey, no!" Sevyn shouts.

When I look back at the stage, Marisa is sliding her thong off her legs. I watch in shock as the dancer takes them from her hand and puts them in his mouth.

"C-Can he do that?" Quinn asks.

"I'm guessing this is the wild part..." I watch Marisa shove her head in the dancer's crotch.

"Um... this escalated quickly," Sevyn says with wide eyes.

I'm speechless as I watch her bow with the dancer before he brings her back to our table. Marisa is laughing hysterically, but stops when she sees the look of shock on our faces.

"What? I just wanted to have some fun." She shrugs, pouring herself another glass of champagne.

"W-We didn't say anything." Quinn stutters.

"No, but you're all looking at me like you don't know me."

"He put your panties... in his mouth." Sevyn enunciates each word. "You're a true legend."

There's a moment of silence before we all laugh hysterically. The shock of the moment dissolves.

"What happens in Vegas stays in Vegas, right?" I ask them as we enjoy the rest of our night.

CHAPTER 13

Acyn's Bachelor Party

E*arlier that same day...*
After saying bye to Harlow and the girls, we await our ride to begin the bachelor party. It pulls up less than a minute later.

"Where to next?" I ask Kyrell as I get into the SUV.

"I can't tell you that." He smirks. "It's a surprise."

"Get off your fucking phone, asshole." Asher kicks Greyson's foot.

"It's Selene," Grey whispers.

"I know," Asher whispers back. "Tell her you forgot to pack your balls."

"Oh, he has some?" Zane scrunches up his face.

I try to hold in a laugh, but Kyrell cracks up, and I let it out. Greyson punches Asher's arm as he lies to Selene and says we're pulling up to our next stop.

"You're whipped, bro. They aren't even that bad." Asher points at Kyrell, Zane, and me. "And they worship the ground those women walk on."

"Yeah, and you're the lonely fucker hunting for pussy every night," Grey quips.

"That's part of the thrill." Asher winks.

"When was the last time you had a girlfriend, Ash?" I ask him, trying to recall if that's ever happened.

"A girlfriend?" he asks incredulously. "Damn, I don't even remember."

"And I thought I had commitment issues." Kyrell chuckles.

"I think Ash has us beat in a lot of things," I reply. Greyson's phone rings again and he stares at it, then back at us. "Man, I respect the love you two have for each other, but she fucking bothers."

"I told you," Ash says in a singsong tone, looking out the window.

"She just misses me." Grey shrugs.

"Mmm... that's not missing," Zane says.

"Yeah, there's a fine line between missing and suffocation," Kyrell adds. "You're a pilot. She should be used to you being gone."

"That's for work. It's different."

"Right... so you're saying she doesn't trust you?" Kyrell asks.

"What? Why would you say that?" Grey looks at him and his ringing phone again.

"You're in Vegas for a bachelor party, and it's known for getting wild. So, I'll repeat myself—there's a fine line between missing and suffocation." Kyrell sighs before looking out the window with a bored expression.

I chuckle, shaking my head because the confused look on Greyson's face lets me know he doesn't get it. "She thinks you're out here to do fuck shit, Grey. That's why she's blowing up your phone. While she may miss you, jealousy is what's really going on here."

Grey looks at his phone thoughtfully for a moment before turning it off and sliding it into his pocket. We weren't saying ignore her, but he'll figure that out in his own time. We can't spell everything out for him. Grey's a good guy. He's the nice one compared to the rest of us, but he's also a pushover and Selene takes advantage of that. Harlow knows she could ask me for the heart in my chest and I'd gladly give it to her, but I know she would willingly give me her own. Grey has been with Selene for three years, and I have yet to see that same energy from her with him.

About twenty minutes later, we pull up to what looks like a racing track.

"Are we watching a race?" I ask with a quirked brow.

"Fuck no. We're racing." Kyrell grins.

"What? For real?" I ask, looking around. I have a love of cars, both old and new.

"Ah, like a kid in a candy store." Zane smiles at me.

"Thank fuck it isn't a strip club." I let out a sigh.

Kyrell pulls his shades down. "Nah, that fuckery is for later—" I let out a rumble of laughter "—but for now you can choose between driving a Ferrari, McLaren, Lamborghini, or whatever else they have here."

Excitement courses through me as we walk into the building for registration. I wasn't expecting this. While Vegas is fun for gambling and partying, I'm happy that we're stepping outside of that box. Kyrell checks us in at registration and then asks for our driver's licenses. The hostess goes over what our driving experience will be like and then we get to choose our cars. I take nearly ten minutes to decide on what to drive because I want to try them all. I finally decide to drive the Lamborghini Huracan Performante.

"Good choice." The hostess smiles.

"Took you long enough." Zane nudges my shoulder.

He chose a Lamborghini, too. Kyrell chose a Ferrari, Asher went with the McLaren, and Greyson decided on a Porsche. Once we're all checked in, we're taken to a classroom to begin our training session with an instructor. They go over the mechanics, how to handle the car on the track, and safety procedures. It's mostly basic, common sense stuff, but it's easy to forget common sense when you're behind the wheel of a dream car.

After the training session, we're taken to a simulator room where we take virtual laps. We won't be driving alone. We're each paired with an instructor who helps us learn the controls of the car and the layout of the track.

"Do you feel comfortable?" the instructor asks me.

"Yes," I reply, eager to get behind the wheel.

"Alright, man. Let's get you suited up," he says.

I thought he was joking when he said we'd get suited up. It's a full racing gear outfit with the jumpsuit and helmet.

"We've got to take a picture," I say to Kyrell once we're in our gear.

"You really are Harlow's other half."

"Oh no, this is for me."

He tosses his head back with laughter. "Bet."

My instructor takes photos of us looking like wannabe bad asses by our chosen cars and as a group. After that's out of the way, it's time to play. I feel like a little kid with how excited I am to get behind the wheel of this Lamborghini. Opening the door, I slide into the seat and buckle up before making the engine rev to life.

My instructor, Lucas, asks, "Are you ready?" His voice resounds through my helmet.

"Hell yeah!"

"Alright," he chuckles. "Slowly pull out onto the track."

I listen to his instructions. There are already others on the track which makes me kind of nervous because I don't want to run into anyone or vice versa.

"Keep on creepin' out..." Lucas says. "You're clear to go."

With those words, adrenaline pumps through my veins. The only other time I've driven a Lamborghini was at Kyrell's place and it was on a residential road. But here on the track I have freedom.

"Up shift here," Lucas says. "Up again. There you go, and up again."

As we come up on the first curve of the track, Lucas guides me around it. "Break real firm... one down shift. Ease off the brakes as you turn. Light throttle for balance around the curves."

Once I get around the first curve of the track, I speed up as I get comfortable and reach speeds up to one hundred and sixty miles per hour on the straighaway. It's an exhilarating experience to have the freedom to drive at speeds you'd get a ticket for. With each lap, I go faster, getting more comfortable with the layout of the track and driving the car with more ease. We're doing ten laps, which sounds like a lot initially, until you're nearly going two hundred miles per hour. I even pass Zane and Asher without killing any of us.

Before I know it, Lucas says, "We'll stay wide and exit at the top."

"Exit?" I ask him, surprised it's already over. I could easily keep going.

He chuckles. "Yeah, those ten laps go by pretty quick."

I pull off the track and park the car, realizing now I want a Lamborghini. We'll see if Harlow will go for that later. I reluctantly get out, thank Lucas, and wait for everyone else to finish their laps. Kyrell is first, Zane second, Asher third, and Greyson last.

"How was that, man?" Kyrell grins, wrapping his arm around my shoulders.

"Shit, I'm wondering if Harlow would be down for me to get a Lambo."

He pats my shoulder. "When you're ready, I know a guy."

"Yeah," Zane says, "you're gonna have to set that meeting up with Titan Tech immediately. I need to drive fast cars regularly."

"This experience really just made me wanna buy shit." Asher agrees.

"When do you not wanna buy shit, Ash?" Greyson asks him.

We all laugh as we head into the building to the lounge. Kyrell gets me a copy of the video footage of me driving and all of us t-shirts. While I love to party as much as the next person, this has been my favorite part of this trip so far. Our driver pulls up in front of the building, and we all pile back into the SUV.

"Alright, let's get some food in our systems before the real fuckery begins." Kyrell rubs his hands together.

I already know this is going to be an interesting fucking night.

Back at the hotel, I head to my room to get ready before we eat. After a shower, I put on distressed dark wash jeans, with a V-neck army green t-shirt, and black Nike Air Max sneakers. For jewelry, I put on a layered gold necklace that Harlow bought me a few months ago and black obsidian crystal bracelets. She says that obsidian protects me from negativity. I'm not sure if that's true, but I rock with it because she's never been wrong about energy, and they look nice. Before I walk out the door, I spray myself with the cologne Harlow got me called Spicebomb.

I head to the guy's room and knock. Greyson opens it seconds later, unsurprisingly on the phone with Selene, who sounds like she's yelling. Poor guy. Asher's pouring himself a drink.

"Do you want one?" he asks, holding up a bottle of whiskey.

"Yeah." I shrug.

"Pour me one too." Zane enters the living room, smoothing his hair out of his face.

"So... how long has Greyson been getting yelled at?" I take a drink of whiskey.

Zane chuckles. "She's still going?"

"God bless the bastard." Asher raises his glass into the air before tipping it back.

I down the rest of mine. "Where's Kyrell?"

"Aw, you missed me?" He appears seconds later. "Looking like this is an art, y'all." He smooths his hands down his shirt.

"Shut the fuck up." I shake my head, laughing.

Asher offers Kyrell a glass of whiskey. He takes it and tosses it back and opens the fridge, pulling out a bag of edibles.

"Where's Greyson?" He hands an edible to each of us.

"Getting bitched at," Zane says, putting the edible in his mouth.

I head back to where the rooms are to find him still arguing with Selene. "Bruh, let's go."

"Selene, look, I love you, but I gotta go. I'll talk to you later tonight," he says, hanging up the phone.

"You good?"

"She's gonna drive me fucking nuts," Greyson growls.

I chuckle. "I think that's how it's supposed to be. Let's go eat and get into whatever Kyrell has planned. Maybe once you're both cooled down, you can talk."

"Yeah." He sighs, following behind me.

"Finally!" Kyrell says when he sees me with Greyson. "Let's roll out."

We decide to go to a restaurant within the hotel since there are countless options to choose from. After we clear enough plates of food for a football team and a few rounds of sake later, we head out to the lobby to start our night. I see her before she sees me, stopping dead in my tracks at the sight of her. Kyrell runs into the back of me.

"What the fu—" he begins before stepping aside and stopping in his tracks too.

All of us stop, staring at Harlow and the girls as they get ready to go off to some male strip show looking like a group of super models. She runs right into me as she digs through her purse. I grab her and pull her flush against my body as she apologizes for running into me.

"Excuse me. I—"

"Look fucking incredible." I finish her sentence for her. "God fucking damn."

She looks up at me with a smile on her face and a million filthy thoughts run through my head.

"Thank you." She simpers.

She's thanking me when I'm the lucky bastard who gets to be with her for the rest of my life. The urge to throw her over my shoulder and carry her up to our suite is strong. I turn to Kyrell to ask him if going out is necessary and see he's feeling up Quinn.

"Do we really have to go out tonight?" I ask him.

"I was wondering the same shit, bruh." Apparently, he has the same thoughts as me as he kisses on Quinn.

I turn my attention back to Harlow as Greyson declares he misses Selene. We may give him shit, but I'd honestly miss Harlow too if she weren't here with me. Sevyn's loud voice interrupts my thoughts of Harlow as she talks to Zane.

"Back up!" Sevyn says to Zane with her hand in his face. "I have no time for this. We have a date with some male strippers. You can have your way with me after."

Marisa cackles. "He just wants to appreciate you lookin' like his last meal."

"Yeah, Sevyn. Let me show you my appreciation." Zane continues to feel her up.

"That's too damn bad! I've been looking forward to this all day. I am going to see sweaty, ripped men, and then I will come back and fuck my husband." Sevyn grabs Harlow's hand, attempting to pull her in the opposite direction, but I keep my arm around her.

Sevyn is always cock blocking someone. I'm sure that's why she's the youngest child. She probably cock blocked our parents from ever having another opportunity. While Asher tries to get with Marisa for the millionth time, I focus my attention on Harlow. My mouth is watering to taste her.

"I can't wait to taste you and hear you scream my name later," I whisper in her ear.

"You should probably know I don't have any panties on," she whispers back.

Her admission causes my arm around her waist to slip, letting them pull her out of my hold and in the opposite direction. She looks at me before they walk out the door, and my dick twitches at the look in her eyes. All I want is to feel her on me.

"So... now that we officially have blue balls aside from Greyson," Kyrell says. "Shall we go to a club?"

"Yeah, fuck it," I say. Not sure that anything will get my mind off of wanting to be balls deep in Harlow right now, but I'll join in.

As we walk outside to wait for our car service, Asher stands next to me.

"Hey, man..."

"Hey..." I side eye him.

"Do you think..." he hesitates, rubbing the back of his neck. "Nah, never mind."

"Do I think what?"

He lets out a sigh, seemingly frustrated with himself. "Marisa man..."

I try to bite back a smile. "Yeah... what about her?"

"She just... I mean, I usually don't have to do much, right? C'mon look at me." He points at his chest and I chuckle. "But she... she..."

Asher and I have been friends since we were thirteen and I've never seen him like this before. It's kind of funny.

"Do you like her, or do you just wanna fuck her?"

"I don't fucking know." He shrugs and falls silent as the SUV pulls up.

"Wow Ash, I think you may actually like someone." I pat his arm and climb into the car.

I can't remember the last time I came to a strip club. When I was young and dumb, I would blow cash at them like I had something to prove. Asher and Greyson were alongside me, doing the same dumb shit. Then we started making real money in our careers and realized there were better things to blow it on.

"Here." Kyrell tries to hand me a stack of cash.

"Nope." I shove my hands into my pockets. "I'm not taking your money."

"Why not? They did." He points to the guys behind him who have cash in their hands.

"I'm not taking your money." I back away from him. Kyrell may have more money than he'll ever know what to do with in his lifetime, but I never want him to feel taken advantage of.

"Will you fucking take the goddamn money?" He waves it in my face. "Look, I enjoy doing shit for people I care about, and I care about you... a lot. You're like a brother to me. Do you think I'd do this shit for any random motherfucker?"

I'm momentarily at a loss for words as I stare at him from behind the cash he's holding in my face. "Uh... no, I don't."

"Then take the fucking money." He shoves it at my chest, and I take it.

"Thanks, Kyrell... I feel the same way about you."

He holds up his hand. "Don't make this fucking weird."

"Alright." I shrug. "I won't... but I love you too," I add and wait for his reaction as I try to keep from laughing.

"Goddammit, Ace!" He gives me a hug, and I toss my head back with laughter.

"Are you two done with your little bromance? I'm trying to see some ass and titties." Asher smirks.

"Don't be jealous," Kyrell says smugly, wrapping his arm around my shoulders as we head inside.

Upon entering the club, a scantily clad woman escorts us to a VIP table. The crowd is going wild for a girl who is dropping it on the pole. Asher still loves this environment and throws some money on the stage as we walk past. When we get to the VIP section, there's a hookah on the table with two buckets of beer and a bottle of Grey Goose.

I sit on one of the chairs and grab a beer. The woman who seated us takes it from my hand.

"Here. Allow me." She smiles, opening it.

"Thanks." I nod as she hands it back to me.

"Anything else I can assist you with?" she asks.

"No, I'm good. They may need help, though." I point to the other guys.

"Let me know if you need anything else." She runs her hand along my shoulder as she walks toward Asher.

Asher is the only one of us who's single and in situations like these, he thoroughly enjoys himself. Sure enough, once she opens his beer, she sits on his lap and is giggling at his terrible jokes. While Asher enjoys the attention, Kyrell, Zane, Greyson, and I smoke some hookah. It's not really my thing, but it gives us something to do other than sitting around and drinking beers.

"So... if I get a lap dance–"

"Sevyn will fucking kill you, Zane." I take a swig of my beer.

Both Kyrell and Greyson crack up.

"Remember when you complimented that girl?" I ask and Zane nods. "Right. Now, take that up ten notches and imagine your funeral."

"Wait, wait, wait. What happened?" Kyrell asks through laughter.

"We went to an event once and for whatever reason, Zane complimented another woman on her dress in front of Sevyn. She had just had the twins and was already feeling some type of way. Then this dumb ass says something like 'oh, that color is nice on you' to the woman. Anyway, I had to hold Sevyn back from tearing him apart. She kicked him out of the house for a week, and he had to stay with me."

"Damn, that big brain of yours only speaks in computer code or what?" Greyson smirks.

"It was a terrible lapse of judgement that she still brings up to this day." Zane hangs his head.

"And you know damn well she'll find out." I point my finger at him. "She's better than the CIA at digging up shit on people. You're better off enjoying a few beers, some hookah, and watching them swing around the pole."

"Would Harlow care?" asks Greyson.

"She doesn't have to care because this doesn't interest me." I shrug. "And..." I take a deep breath. "She would wipe me from the face of this earth."

Kyrell cracks up. "I was about to say."

Some dancers enter our section and Zane immediately tenses. I can tell he's already mentally apologizing to Sevyn from the look on his face. One of them gets close to talk to him and he drops his beer at her feet. Kyrell and I laugh hysterically as he profusely apologizes and tries to clean it up.

"My name's Sasha. Would you like a dance?" an overly sweet voice asks.

I turn to see a dancer standing in front of me. I hadn't noticed her because I was too busy laughing at Zane's conundrum.

"Oh, nah. I'm—"

Before I can finish my sentence, she whips her glitter covered hair in my face. Hitting my eye and giving me a mouthful. I gag and am momentarily blinded. Her head connects with the glass beer bottle in my hand, causing it to clatter to the ground.

"Fucking shit!" I grab my eye while pulling strands of hair out of my mouth.

I can hear Kyrell's laughter over the blaring music. The dancer pops her head back up, and from what I can see with my good eye, she looks mortified.

"Oh my God!" she gasps. "I am so sorry about that. I didn't mean—I'm so sorry. It's my first night. I just—are you okay?"

She reaches out to touch me, and I move away from her, nearly tipping over the chair. "I'm fine," I say, still holding my stinging eye. She's just trying to do her job, albeit she's terrible at it, but I still have the urge to tell her to get the fuck away from me.

"I—I can get you guys another bucket of beer, or maybe you'd want to go to a private room?"

"No, no, no!" I hold my hands up. "No private room. It's fine. I'm good. We're good."

She stands there, staring at me, and tears well in her eyes. I glance at Kyrell, who can barely breathe from laughing so hard, and he shrugs.

"Uh... it's okay. It was an accident..."

"I don't want to get fired. I need this job." She sobs.

I stare at her in disbelief, wondering how this escalated so quickly. Zane is looking at me, wondering what I'll do next. While Greyson is rolling on the couch laughing. I let out an exasperated sigh. "Look, I'm sure worse shit happens here. It was an accident. No harm done." I shrug with my vision still blurry in my right eye.

I dig in my pocket for some bills and hand it to her. "Shit happens."

"Are you serious?" she looks down at the cash in her hand.

"Yes." I am so fucking serious. Even if she could dance, I don't want her near me. She takes a step toward me, and I put my hands out in hopes she won't come any closer.

She stops in her tracks. "Thank you," she whispers before turning around and practically running out of our section.

I shake my head, rubbing my eye, and turn my attention back to Kyrell. "I appreciate the effort, but this definitely isn't my scene anymore."

"To be honest, mine either, but that shit was hilarious!" He's still laughing with Greyson and Zane.

Sucking my teeth, I glare at him. "Then what the fuck are we here for?"

"It's Vegas and a bachelor party." He shrugs. "It seemed fitting."

I can't help but laugh. "If I have any damage to my eye, you're footing the bill."

"Bruh, she nearly knocked herself out on that bottle!" Kyrell exclaims. "I kind of felt bad for laughing, but fuck. And it's her first night too! She's got a long road ahead of her."

"Yeah, she'll feel that tomorrow," I say as my vision clears.

"Wanna go back to the hotel and hit up the casino? The night is young, and I refuse for it to end at," he glances at his watch, "midnight."

We've only been here for an hour, but the smoke, flashing lights, and blaring music are getting to me. "Yeah, that's more my tempo."

I glance at Asher, who is in the corner with two women dancing on his lap.

"Aye," I say to Asher. "Are you staying?"

"You're done already?" he asks with his eyes trained on the dancer's ass.

"This doesn't do it for me anymore. You know that."

"It's your party. I'll follow whatever you wanna do. I can find a girl to dance on my belt anywhere." He smirks. "Ladies, ladies, I've thoroughly enjoyed all you've given me tonight." He stands up and slides more cash into their bras and panties.

"Such a gentleman." I smirk.

"Damn, partying isn't as fun when you're the only one enjoying all the play."

"Nah, partying loses its appeal when your priorities change," Kyrell says, taking a final drag on the hookah.

"I enjoy my freedom," Asher says.

"Is it really freedom if you're fucking lonely, though?" Kyrell asks him.

For whatever reason, Kyrell gets away with saying the rawest shit to people. If Greyson or I had said that to Asher, I think he would want to fight. Kyrell is nonchalant in the way he says things and truly means no harm. He's like Yoda. Asher stares at him for a moment. Probably deciding whether or not he wants to argue. He must decide against it because he scrolls through his phone in silence. We head outside to wait for our car service, and I open up Instagram to stalk Harlow. She posted a story two minutes ago, and it's of a very drunk Sevyn and Marisa singing at the top of her lungs. When the camera flips to her, she's laughing at them with Quinn.

"Sevyn is gone with the fucking wind," I say to Zane, showing him the video.

"Yep... that's my wife." He grins.

We pile into the SUV and head back to the hotel to blow some cash before we call it a night.

CHAPTER 14

Acyn

After winning a jackpot on a slot machine, I head up to the suite to find Harlow. Today was an unforgettable experience in many ways. Winning some money is the perfect way to end the night. Well... I can actually think of a better way.

I see her silhouette on the balcony illuminated by the Vegas lights. While I enjoyed today, the only person I want to spend time with is right in front of me.

"Sunshine..." I place my hands on her hips and kiss her neck.

She leans into me and smiles. "I felt you before I saw you."

I wrap my arms around her shoulders, resting my chin on top of her head, and watch the fountain dance below us as the lights change colors. "Did you have a good night?"

She places her hands on my forearms. "It was fun. Marisa took off her panties, and the dancer put them in his mouth. She nearly went home with him at the end of the show. Quinn and I had to talk her out of it while Sevyn cheered her on."

I laugh. "That sounds like something Sevyn would do."

"Yeah, they're in the room now... hopefully sleeping. Poor Quinn had to help me get them both back to the room."

"You could've called us. Zane would've picked up Sevyn's drunk ass."

"No." she turns around to face me. "We got them up here..." Her voice trails off as her brow furrows. "Why is there glitter in your beard? And your right eye looks... red."

"Oh... uh. A stripper—" her eyes narrow "—wait, let me finish. A stripper whipped her hair in my face, nearly blinding me. She almost knocked herself out too when she hit the side of her head on the beer bottle I was holding with her aggressive ass hair flip. Then she started crying, telling me it was her first night dancing." I let out a sigh. "Your husband isn't about that life no more."

She glares at me before she tosses her head back with laughter. "Please tell me you tipped her!"

"I did out of fear she'd come near me again." Harlow laughs harder. "Yeah, yeah. Hilarious." I smirk. "What else did you get into?"

"Me?" she asks, swallowing. "Oh ya know, just a show with the girls... got carried up on stage by a stripper, possibly flashed hundreds of people my vagina, and then I got a lap dance from him in a tiny blue speedo before I nearly died of embarrassment. Your wife isn't about that life either and apparently never was."

"You got a lap dance." I raise my brow, "And I got blinded? Something isn't right."

She buries her face in my chest, laughing, and wraps her arms around my middle. "I'll give you a lap dance," she purrs, looking up at me.

"Mmm... I've only had one thought all night." I turn her around, grabbing her hips, and pulling her flush against me. I wrap my hand around her neck and kiss it while my other hand squeezes her breast. A moan spills from her lips that makes my dick twitch.

"Being inside you has been my only thought all night," I whisper in her ear before grazing my teeth along her neck.

Rucking up her skirt, I shove my hand between her legs, rubbing my fingers along her wetness. She grips the balcony railing, spreading her legs apart for me as she rests her head against my chest, melting into my touch. Her wetness drips down my fingers when I dip them inside of her warmth. Pulling them out, I rub her clit in slow circles, coaxing her to unravel for me as I unbutton my pants with my free hand. Once they're undone, I caress her curves that I've committed to memory. Her skin feels like velvet beneath my fingertips. Brushing her hair aside, I trail kisses along her shoulder and across her back and see goose bumps break out on her skin as she shivers.

"Acyn..." she whimpers as her knees buckle and she grips the railing a little tighter. I wrap my arm around her waist to keep her steady. Her soft moans become louder, and she makes a strangled noise.

"Don't hold back, Sunshine. I want to hear you call out my name."

She cums, calling out my name. I keep one hand on her clit while gripping the back of her neck and bending her forward with my other hand. As she's cumming, I bury myself in her wetness. Her breath hitches, and I groan at the feel of her tight pussy around my dick. She hikes her skirt further up her hips, giving me a perfect view of her ass cheeks bouncing on my dick as I pound into her. I move my hand from between her legs to her hip and grab a fistful of her hair with my other.

"Harder, Acyn!" she pants, throwing it back for me.

I grab both of her hips and thrust into her, giving her what she wants and I need.

"Take all this dick, baby," I growl.

Her pussy puts my dick in a vise as she cums for me again. The tension that has been building all day finally snaps. I topple over the edge, holding onto her, seeing stars in my eyes as my climax shivers through me, and my cum spills into her. My thrusts slow as I ride out my orgasm. I bury myself deep inside her before leaning forward and kissing her back.

"I never thought I'd be cumming while enjoying this view," she says hoarsely, leaning forward and resting her head on the balcony railing.

"I'm all about adding to the experience," I say, pulling out of her and smacking her ass before covering it with her skirt.

She straightens up and turns around to face me, wrapping her arms around my neck. "Wanna stay up the rest of the night drinking champagne and watch the sunrise?"

"I've got the goods." I pull a container with a pre-rolled joint out of my pocket that Kyrell gave me earlier.

"You're speaking to my heart." She smiles, and I kiss her lips.

We spend the last couple of hours of the night stretched out on a lounge chair, talking, sharing a joint, and finishing off a bottle of champagne until the sun rises.

Harlow

Shortly after sunrise, I fell asleep laying on Acyn's chest that's now covered in my drool. Sitting up, I wipe the side of my mouth, and Acyn stirs. He throws his arm over his eyes and pulls me back on top of him.

"What time is it?" he asks in a raspy, deep tone.

"Uh..." I fumble around in his back pockets to pull out his phone. "It's just past noon."

"I'm fucking starving," he mumbles with his eyes still closed.

"Me too. Should we order room service and then we can get our shit together to see what everyone else is doing?"

"I'd be surprised if anyone is even coherent right now."

"Actually, I know for sure Quinn is." She's the only one who couldn't get drunk.

"Hit her up. If Kyrell's awake, then we can get some food with them. Unless you wanted to have breakfast in bed?"

"We can see who else is up because I'm sure we're not the only ones starving."

I climb off Acyn to find my phone sitting on the table next to my clutch. Grabbing it, I head to the bathroom and call Quinn as I turn on the shower. She picks up on the second ring.

"You're alive," she says happily.

"Barely," I say groggily. "Have you eaten?"

"I had a smoothie, but Kyrell just woke up and said he needs food."

"Is anyone else up?"

"Nope. Just Ky and I."

"Do you wanna go get food together?"

"Of course. I'll tell Kyrell. Want to meet in the lobby?"

"Yeah, give us twenty minutes to shower and get our shit together.

"Sounds good. See ya soon."

I hang up the phone, strip out of my clothes, and step into the shower. Acyn comes in after me, pressing me up against the shower wall.

"I told them..." he kisses me, "twenty..." he kisses me again, "minutes."

"Then we better be quick, Sunshine."

We head back up to the suites after lunch. Quinn and I decide to wake up the girls. Sevyn is in the shower, but Marisa is nowhere to be found. Her bag and phone are where we left them last night on the counter.

"Have you seen Marisa?" I ask Sevyn as she comes out of the shower, drying her hair.

"No, to be honest, I don't remember much after we got food last night."

Quinn laughs. "I bet you don't. We had to carry you back up here."

"I'm sorry." She cringes. "She's not in her room?"

"No. Her bag and phone are still here, too."

"Maybe she went out to grab some coffee or something." Sevyn sits at the table to apply her makeup.

"Mmm... I don't know. I think she would've said something." Quinn says.

"What if something happened to her?" I look around the room.

Sevyn sucks her teeth. "Please, I know she was just as drunk as I was. If she went anywhere, she didn't go far."

"She has a point, Harls. Let's ask the guys if they saw her."

We head across the hall to the guys' suite. Kyrell and Acyn are watching something on TV when we enter the room.

"Have either of you seen Marisa?" Standing in front of them, I block their view.

"No. Is she not in her room?" Kyrell asks.

"She isn't," Quinn says, looking around the suite.

"Oh my God. What if something happened to her? We shouldn't have left her alone." I pace the room. "Where could she have even gone? She was shitfaced."

"Chill, Sunshine. This isn't an unsolved mysteries episode."

"No," I point my finger at him. "But they always start like this."

"Normally I'd think Harls was being dramatic," Quinn says. "But she left her phone in the room."

Marisa rarely goes anywhere without her phone. I left it on the counter last night because she has a history of sending drunk calls and texts. But even then, she would've grabbed her phone.

"Did you see her after we carried her to the room?"

"No, I spent the night here with Kyrell. I'm actually impressed she could get up after we got her in bed."

"Marisa can hold her alcohol." I sit on the armrest next to Acyn on the couch. "It's not like her to not say anything, though."

"Let's ask the other guys." Acyn says.

Zane enters the living room. "What'd I miss?"

"Did you see Marisa last night or this morning?" Acyn asks.

"No... I probably wouldn't remember, anyway. I was high and drunk by the time we got back to the room. Went straight to bed." He shrugs, leaning against the counter as he twists the cap off a bottle of water.

"You sound exactly like Sevyn." Quinn smirks.

"We're married for a reason." He smiles before downing the bottle of water. "Maybe Grey saw her? Ash was talking to some girls at the casino the last time I saw him. I don't even know if he came back last night."

"I can—" Kyrell starts but is interrupted by the door opening.

Greyson comes into the suite, dripping sweat. He stops in his tracks, slowly removing his earbuds as we look at him. "Um... am I gonna need a lawyer?" he asks.

"Nah, we're just trying to find Marisa," Kyrell says. "Although we're not sure she's lost. And why the fuck are you working out on vacation?"

"For real, bruh, why?" Zane asks.

"Selene," Grey grumbles.

"Did you happen to see Marisa while you were out?" Acyn asks Greyson.

"Marisa? No. The last time I saw her was with you two last night," Greyson says, pointing at Quinn and me.

The door of the suite opens again. I hold my breath, hoping it's Marisa. "Oh, it's just you," I say as Sevyn appears.

"Damn, what a warm welcome." She laughs and heads for Zane, giving him a kiss. "Still haven't found our girl, yet? I'm sure she's fine."

"No, we—"

"For the love of god, can you guys keep it down? Some of us have hangovers," Asher says as comes out of his room, pulling a shirt over his head.

"Have you seen Marisa?" Acyn asks. "None of us have seen her."

"Have I seen Marisa?" He smirks. "Have I seen—Risa, love!" he hollers from where he's standing. My eyes widen as I look at him and then at Quinn, who looks just as shocked as I do. "Come out here so they can see you're alive and well!"

It's silent as we all look at each other in disbelief that this is actually happening.

"Risa?" Sevyn asks. "Is Risa Maris—"

"I'm gonna fucking kill you, Ash!" Marisa screams and seconds later she comes out wielding her stiletto from last night dressed in Asher's sweats and t-shirt.

Asher jumps over the back of the couch, trying to get away from her as he laughs.

"They... slept together?" Quinn gasps as we watch Marisa attempt to wipe Asher off the face of the earth.

"I'm better off missing than admitting to ever having fucked you!" She lunges at him and smacks him with her shoe. Asher's faster and runs aways from her to hide behind Kyrell and Acyn who are laughing hysterically. They move to the side.

"You did this to yourself, man." Acyn laughs.

"Oh, c'mon baby," Asher says as he stands behind a chair, holding his hand out in front of him. "You know you needed the release as much as I did."

Marisa grabs the TV remote off the couch and hurls it at him. He isn't fast enough for her anger, and it hits him square in the forehead.

"Fuck!" he shouts, falling to his knees. "You know I like it rough." He groans, rolling around on the floor, holding his forehead.

Zane and Sevyn are laughing so hard they're wheezing. Greyson comes out of the bathroom with his toothbrush hanging out of his mouth, eyes wide, wondering what the hell he missed. Acyn and Kyrell haven't stopped laughing since Marisa hit Asher with her stiletto. And I'm in shock, along with Quinn, that Marisa actually slept with him after all the shit she talked.

"I can't fucking stand you!" Marisa screams. "I told you not to say shit! Do you wanna tell them how you lasted less than a minute the first round?"

"Wait... you fucked him more than once?" I ask, biting back a smile.

"I had to," she says defensively, "so I could get off properly."

"Don't lie on my dick, Risa!" Asher yells, getting up off the floor. He seems more pissed off about her saying he lasted only a minute than the fact she just hit him with the remote. "I had you saying my name like I'm your God." He ducks behind the couch as she hurls her shoe at him. She misses this time. "Just admit you enjoyed yourself!"

Quinn turns to me. "He has a nickname for her?"

"I've had better!" Marisa screams before I can answer.

Quinn, Sevyn, and I exchange a look, knowing damn well that's a lie.

"Really?" Asher smirks. "I couldn't tell from the way I just made you cum for me less than twenty minutes ago."

"Um..." I say, unsure of what to do. Quinn looks at me, cringing, and shrugs.

"This is better than reality TV," Zane says.

"Hell yeah, it is." Kyrell laughs.

"Keep your fucking trap shut!" Marisa screams at him, and I step in front of her before she can lunge at him again. Her chest is heaving, and I imagine this is what murder looks like in someone's eyes.

"Marisa..." I grab the sides of her face. "Look at me. You've gotta calm down. It already happened. Let's go back to our room, yeah? We can talk shit about Asher."

"Hey!" Asher says from behind me.

"Say another fucking word, Asher, and I swear to the Devil and all things unholy, I will shove that stiletto up your ass," I say to him without taking my eyes off her. "Marisa, let's go."

"I—" Asher begins.

"Leave it, Ash." Acyn warns him. "You've said enough."

"You're a real dick, Asher. You know that?" Quinn says, wrapping her arm around Marisa and following us out the door.

"It was just for—"

"Some shit isn't just for fun, Asher." I scoff, rolling my eyes. "Not everyone pretends to be devoid of emotion and disconnected like you."

I guide Marisa out the door with Quinn on her other side and Sevyn right behind us. It was funny at first until Asher kept going and putting intimate details out there for all of us to hear. When we're out in the hallway, Marisa turns around and hugs me. She lets out a sigh and pulls Quinn into the hug.

"Get in here, bitch." Marisa says to Sevyn. She laughs and wraps her arms around us all. "Fucking Vegas. Thanks for getting me out of there, but can I tell you guys a secret?"

"I—I'm not sure what other secrets you're withholding that Asher didn't just put on the table..." I say, pulling away from her and opening the door to their suite.

"Yeah... what more are you not saying?" Quinn asks.

"I hate to admit it..." Marisa lets out an exasperated sigh, "but Asher has a big dick, and he knows how to use it."

We fall into a fit of laughter as I kick the door shut behind us.

CHAPTER 15

Harlow

That afternoon, I learn more about Asher than I ever cared to. It's one of those things you don't want to know, but you're curious about how it happened.

"Wait... so it's clear the dick was phenomenal, but how did you end up in his bed in the first place?" I ask as we sit huddled on the couch after ordering some snacks and room service.

"I woke up dying of thirst, and there was no ice. When I went out to the ice machine, Asher was coming down the hallway. Our casual conversation turned into him taking me to his bed." She shrugs, putting a piece of chicken into her mouth.

"I feel this has been building for a while," Quinn says.

"Yeah... that back and forth between you guys was bound to explode," Sevyn adds.

"He's arrogant, but... he's also so goddamn sexy. With those full, soft lips, honey brown eyes, smooth brown skin, and his muscles... the muscles!" She clutches her chest. "His abs are just," she does a chef's kiss motion with her hand, "and then his face. Why are all the gorgeous men assholes?"

"You're gonna fuck him again, aren't you?" I snort with laughter. Sevyn and Quinn laugh hysterically.

"Look, I'm not gonna make a liar out of myself by saying yes or no. It's on a case-by-case basis at this point," she says, not looking any of us in the face.

"If you wanna fuck him, fuck him! We support you!" Quinn says. "Kyrell and I started out in a friend's with benefits situation. And now..." she puts her hands on her belly.

Marisa looks at her with wide eyes. "I need to buy Plan B now that you mention it."

I fall back onto the bed, cracking up. "For fuck's sake, Marisa!"

"Aye, at least get him to pay for it," Sevyn says with laughter.

"Good idea, Sev." Marisa points at her. "Where's my phone?"

I sit on Acyn's lap, looking at all the pictures we took as we wait to board our flight. For our last night in Vegas, we went to dinner and a Cirque du Soleil show. It was the perfect way to end our weekend. If we hadn't eloped, I'm not sure we would've been able to enjoy this trip as much as we did. It was a relief to enjoy the time with our friends and not have the wedding looming in the back of my mind. Even Acyn's grumpy ass is looking forward to the reception.

Greyson was able to get us some deeply discounted tickets since he's a pilot, which means we're flying first class. They call for us to board and Acyn grabs our things. Quinn and Kyrell are coming back to Seattle with us so Quinn can help me with reception stuff. Marisa wanted to come too but has a yoga training that she's teaching the first half of the week. She'll be there a few days before the reception. Asher had to get back to L.A. for business meetings but will arrive the same day as Marisa. It'll be interesting to see what happens with those two. If anything more even happens at all.

We settle into our seats, and I rest my head on Acyn's shoulder. Vacations are always exhausting even if they are relaxed. This was our first time in Vegas, and I know it won't be our last. There's too much to do here to fit it all into a weekend. Acyn holds a piece of paper out to me as the plane takes off. I grab it from his hand and realize it's a check. My eyes meet his and he has his signature lopsided grin on his face. I look at the check in my hand and read the number.

"Are you—" I slide my sunglasses up to the top of my head. "Is this... legal?"

"Yes, I don't know who does illegal business with checks."

"You have a point. But... ten grand is a lot. Did you win this at your bachelor party?"

"Yeah, after the strip club incident, we hit up the casino. I placed a $4 bet on a slot machine. Mind you, I had lost nearly a grand before that."

I snort with laughter. "Does the grand matter when you won ten?"

"No, but it sucks losing money. You know how I am."

Acyn is excellent with money management. He's not filthy rich, but money isn't something he has to worry about. He calls it comfortable. I call it well off.

"What are you gonna do with it?" I ask.

"We, Sunshine. Always we." He interlaces his fingers with mine and kisses the back of my hand.

I smile as butterflies ignite in my stomach. "What are we doing with it?"

"We talked about building a house and—"

I gasp, covering my mouth. "We're gonna do it? Now? Like as in soon?"

"Yeah, well, if you still want to."

"I love our house, but I would love for us to build one together."

"Let's do it then, Sunshine."

I squeal, wrapping my arms around his neck. After watching some home improvement shows after we first got engaged, I told him it would be fun to build our own house someday. Acyn bought the home we live in before we met with the idea he'd get married and have a family in the future. Now we're married, and I could see us raising a family there, but building a house from the ground up together would be a beautiful legacy. Acyn suggested we open a savings account specifically for this house we'd "someday" build. Over the past year, we've been putting money into it and now someday is here.

"You make all my dreams come true." I kiss him.

"Make sure you build a room for me." Kyrell smirks.

Quinn laughs. "Let them have their moment."

"Where's my house, Zane?" Sevyn asks.

"We have one that you—" Zane sighs, resting his head against the seat. "Thanks for setting such a high bar for the rest of us, Ace. I always appreciate it." He smirks.

After a hectic morning at work, I finally take a moment to sit down at my desk and breathe. My phone rings. I let out a sigh, wishing for a moment of calm. Glancing at the screen, I see that it's Gloria.

"Hi, Gloria."

"Good morning, love. How was your trip?"

"Good." I ease back in my chair. "Acyn and I had an amazing time with our friends."

"I'm happy to hear that," she says warmly. "Are you guys ready for the reception?"

"Yeah." I let out a yawn. "We just need to go over who RSVP'd. I'm going to do that later today when I get a moment."

She hesitates. "If you want—well, never mind. I only wanted to call to check in on you."

Despite going with a small, intimate party, there's still a lot to do. Looking at my desk, I can already tell it's going to be a later night then usual as I prepare to be gone for two weeks.

"Gloria... if you're not busy, I'd love to have some help this week with preparations. Quinn—"

"Done!" she says, and I chuckle. "Whatever you need, consider it done."

Things may have been rocky with the original wedding plans, but I want her to be involved. With her, Quinn, Sevyn, and Ava—I know I won't have to worry about a thing.

"Thank you so much, Gloria. There's more to do than I expected before we leave for our honeymoon."

"You two are leaving right after the reception?"

"Yes, we'll catch our flight about three hours after it ends. So straight to the airport after." I make a mental note to begin packing our things tonight.

"No pressure, but I'm hoping for more grand babies soon."

I chuckle, biting my lip. "I'll be sure to tell Acyn."

"Alright, darling. I'll keep you updated. Love you."

"Love you too."

Hanging up the phone, I toss it on the desk. I got my IUD removed shortly after our engagement party. Not because we wanted to have a baby, initially, but because it was time to get it replaced. When I told Acyn about it, we talked about kids and when we wanted to have them. We realized there's nothing holding us back. Instead of getting a new IUD put in, I decided to stop birth control. The doctor told me it could take a few months for me to get pregnant. We decided if it happens, it happens. But it's been more than a few months and in the back of my mind, I can't help but wonder if we'll ever have kids. I think I'd be more worried if I were tracking my fertility and we were actively trying to get pregnant. But it's not something I think about until someone mentions us having kids. Then I quietly obsess about it for a while before it falls into the back of my mind again.

Like right now, as Acyn strides into my studio with Kyrell at his side. A smile pulls at my lips. "To what do I owe this pleasure?"

"Mom said you sounded stressed and scolded me for not helping."

"Don't you have work to do?" Getting up from my seat, I give him a kiss.

"Do you think she gives a damn about that?" He imitates her voice. "You can't just sit back and let her do the work, Acyn."

I snort with laughter as I give Kyrell a hug. Gloria knows Acyn spoils me, but she never misses a chance to tell him if she thinks he's falling short.

"And I brought food." Kyrell places a bag on my desk.

I grab the bag and the smell of tacos wafts out of it. "You brought me tacos? I love you forever."

"I know." Kyrell grins, taking a seat and propping his feet up on the desk.

"He didn't even get those." Acyn side eyes Kyrell.

"Can't let me have anything, can you Ace?" He shakes his head. "You've already married her. Let me have glory for the tacos."

"Not sure you've noticed, but Acyn has a bit of a sharing problem."

"Well shit, so do I. What's up?" Kyrell throws his hands up in the air. "If we want to get technical, I was here first."

I roll my eyes, taking a seat on the couch. "You two are a mess."

Acyn knocks Kyrell's feet off the desk before he joins me on the couch. They fight like brothers and, to be honest, it's cute and makes my heart skip a beat.

He wraps his arm around my shoulder as I take a bite of taco. "Since my mom told me I'm a mediocre husband, do you need help with anything?"

I chuckle. "No, it's decorations and last-minute things for the reception. I don't think either of you wants to help with that."

"I feel I should tell you I'll help you with anything here, but you also know me well enough to know decorating isn't my forte."

"Yeah, it's a hard pass for me, too," Kyrell says, fiddling with things on my desk.

"Wow, you guys are so helpful," I tease.

"Does support count?" Acyn grins.

"It does. And that's all I need. I'm not worried about it. There's just a lot to do here before we leave."

"Do you need me to be your assistant for the day?" Kyrell flashes me a smile. "Models love me."

"Not sure how Quinn got past your arrogance, but God bless her," I say, and Acyn lets out a rumble of laughter.

"She knows all my toxic traits and loves me, anyway." He shrugs.

"Actually... if you want to assist me today, that would be great. I have a shoot with some babies. It could be good practice."

"Whatever you need, Harls."

"I really wish I could stay to see this, but I've gotta run back to my shop. Elijah is stopping by."

"Aw, Elijah!" I smile. "Tell him I said hi and he better be coming to the reception."

Elijah has been getting tatted up by Acyn since he was an apprentice. He is also the reason he nearly missed my twenty-fourth birthday, and Acyn makes sure to never let him forget that.

"I think he's afraid of you and wouldn't dare miss it." He kisses me and turns to Kyrell. "Don't make the babies cry, alright?"

"Fuck you. Children love me." Kyrell tries to punch Acyn's arm, but he dodges it.

"Later, Sunshine." He gives me a two-finger salute before leaving.

I finish eating my tacos. As I'm chewing, a thought occurs to me, "Kyrell, have you ever been around babies?"

He's been around Sevyn's kids, but they're older and do a lot for themselves. Kids under the age of one are entirely different. They're into everything. Basically a drunk, tiny, carefree human.

"Nah." He shrugs. "But how hard can it be?"

I toss my head back with laughter. "This is going to be interesting."

After a few hours of giggling, crying, and sometimes screaming babies, Kyrell beelines for the bathroom. I follow close behind him.

"Is that all they do?" Kyrell asks me as he vigorously scrubs his Gucci shirt with a wet cloth. "Shit, puke, laugh, and repeat?"

I laugh hysterically as he makes the shit stain on his shirt worse the more he rubs. One baby had a blowout in the middle of the shoot, and Kyrell was holding him.

He throws the towel into the sink. "Fuck. This is ruined. You knew this was going to happen, didn't you?" He smiles as he slips his shirt over his head.

Holding my stomach, I take in a deep breath and try to control my laughter. "How would I know a baby was going to poop on you?"

"I don't know. You seemed a little too eager to see me struggle with those babies."

"I thought your confidence would carry you through like it always does."

"Damn." He scratches his jaw, letting out a sigh. "I'm fucked, aren't I?"

"No! You're gonna be a great dad. Your kid is lucky as hell."

His carefree demeanor falters as his brow furrows. "Harls... I'm gonna be fucked up for the rest of my life."

"Is that how you see yourself? Fucked up?"

He crosses his arms, shrugging his shoulders. "Yeah... it is. Some days are alright and some days I miss my dad so much that getting out of bed is the last thing I wanna do."

After losing his dad only months ago, Kyrell has been struggling to keep his head above water. He's doing better than he was, but that doesn't mean it's easier. We unfortunately have losing our parents in common. I understand what he's going through on a soul level.

"Kyrell, you need to allow yourself some grace. You can have good days and shit days. And fuck anyone who says otherwise. You got people around you who can ease the load when it feels like it's too much. But I can guarantee you, no one sees you as fucked up." I lean against the counter next to him. "That's just a lie you told yourself."

"I have a tendency to do that." He chuckles.

"You know what?" I nudge his arm.

"What?"

"Your baby will love you as you are. Just like Quinn does. Like we all do."

He takes a deep breath. "Thanks, Harls." His eyes meet mine. "I'd hate to know where I'd be without you."

"We'd both be lost at sea. I'm always here for you, and I love you." I hug him and pull away, covering my nose. "You smell like baby puke and poop."

"I can't fucking help it." He laughs.

"C'mon, you're in need of a shower. Thanks for helping me today. It was fun to hang out with you."

"Anything you need, Harls." He wraps his arm around my neck as we head out to my car.

CHAPTER 16

Harlow

A fter the craziness of the week, I'm happy to be sprawled out on my dad's couch as he cooks lunch for us. I scheduled a half day because I thought I'd be running around taking care of last-minute wedding preparations. True to her word, Gloria handled everything with the help of Quinn, Sevyn, Marisa, and Ava. Since we'll be gone for two weeks, I worked late every night and am happy to have the rest of the day to breathe. Well... almost the rest of the day. One would think Vegas would've been enough partying, but our friends planned a get together tonight before our reception tomorrow.

I hear the front door open and Acyn appears a few seconds later with a small black bag in his hand. He presses a kiss to my forehead.

"Ooo, what did you get me?" I reach for the bag.

He moves it behind his back. "Not shit."

I cackle. "Damn! Why are you so aggressive?"

"I'm not." He grins as he sits on the couch. "It's something your dad asked me to pick up."

"From where?" I sit up, reaching for it again.

He presses the palm of his hand to my forehead. "Nowhere, nosy!"

I laugh, falling back against the couch. "You two are keeping secrets, and I intend to find out what they are."

"Good luck with that, Sunshine." He pulls my legs onto his lap. "Where's Felix?"

"Cooking. You know him, always making us some new recipe he found online." I smile.

He nods his head. "Are you ready for tonight?"

"I wanna know whose idea it was to throw a party the night before the reception."

"Take a wild guess."

"I know it wasn't Kyrell, so it had to be Asher."

"Bingo." He chuckles. "He'll use any occasion to be in the center of a party."

I groan. "Is this happening at our place?"

"I could tell him to have it at Greyson's, so we don't have to deal with the cleanup. That's where everyone's at right now, anyway."

"I love the way your mind works."

He pulls his phone out of his pocket and types out a text and his phone chimes a second later with a response. "Grey says he knows what we're doing, but he supports it."

I snort with laughter. "He's the real MVP."

My dad appears in the living room. "Ah, Ace, you're here." He smiles as Acyn gets up to give him a hug. "Did they have it?" my dad asks in a hushed tone.

"Yeah." He hands him the bag.

He glances at it before patting Acyn on the shoulder and giving him another hug. "Thank you."

"Just pretend I'm not here." I sit up on the couch.

They turn toward me, and Acyn has a glimmer in his eye. He's enjoying this way too much.

"Let's eat first, then we'll get to what's in the bag." My dad smiles warmly.

I roll my eyes at Acyn, who chuckles and interlaces his fingers with mine as we walk into the kitchen. My annoyance with them is quickly forgotten when the smells of what my dad has been cooking hits my nose and makes my mouth water.

"Whatever you made smells delicious."

"Philly cheesesteaks. You'll have to let me know how it tastes," he says as we sit down at the table. "Are you two ready for tomorrow?"

"Yes," we answer in unison and laugh.

"Good." My dad chuckles. "I'm looking forward to it."

I grab my sandwich from the plate. "What will you be up to while we're gone?"

"I'm back to teaching. I'll be busier than I probably care to be, but I enjoy it."

"It makes me happy that you found something you enjoy doing." I smile at him.

"Me too, kiddo," he says before taking a bite of his sandwich.

I take a bite of my own, and it tastes better than it smells. "Mmmm..." I close my eyes. "This is perfection. We're gonna have to steal this recipe." I say to Acyn.

"Be my guest. Are you guys all packed for your trip?" my dad asks.

"Surprisingly, Harlow finished packing a few days ago." Acyn smirks.

"What?" my dad asks, shocked. "She did?"

"I'm not that bad, you guys." I roll my eyes. "We're going across the world. I had to be sure we're prepared."

Again, clothes aren't really on the agenda for the honeymoon, but I won't write off the possibility of sightseeing while we're there. We have access to a private beach and the bungalow has a butler and everything we'll need while we're there. It'll be two weeks of sun and healthy doses of my husband. Absolute bliss.

We clear our plates, and I insist on my dad letting Acyn and me clean up while he heads to the living room to relax. It doesn't take us long before we join him. He's watching *Lord of the Rings* kicked back in his recliner. It's the same one my mom got him the Christmas before she passed. He's kept it in wonderful condition over the years.

"I wanted to give you something." He sits up and grabs the little black bag Acyn wouldn't let me near, holding it out to me.

I take it from him and sit down on the couch. Acyn makes himself comfortable beside me. "Thank you, Dad." I smile.

The bag is tied at the top with a black velvet ribbon. I recognize the name 'Asterin' scrawled across the bag in gold. It's the jewelry shop where Acyn got my wedding ring custom designed. I pull a small box out and open it.

"Y-You..." My voice trails off as I glance at him, then back at the box. My vision blurs as tears pool in my eyes. I'm hesitant to touch the glinting contents. "I thought... it was still with her."

"When you and mom got in that accident..." He takes a steadying breath. I focus on him, wiping the tears from my cheeks. "They took off all her jewelry and gave it to me after... after she passed. I remember while I waited for you to wake up, all I could do was stare at this bag of her of her blood stained jewelry... remembering where each piece came from." He wipes away his tears. "I realized in that moment all you'd have are memories of her... pieces of her. Her necklaces I gave to you because—"

"I asked for them." When I was thirteen, I asked my dad if I could have her necklaces. I rarely take them off. There are four. All gold and varying lengths, with different gems and chains. The pieces are timeless, like my mom.

"Yes," he smiles. "But her wedding ring... I wasn't sure whether or not to bury her with it. In the end, I kept it because I felt she would've wanted you to have it for when you got married someday. Just like her wedding dress. Acyn helped with your ring size and got it resized for me. I know how you feel about your wedding ring—" I sniffle and laugh because I protect it with my life "—so I had it resized to fit on the ring finger of your right hand."

I get up and hug him tightly. There are no words to be said, only emotions to be felt. This is the most beautiful gift my dad could've possibly given me.

"Thank you, Dad. I love you."

"I love you too, kiddo. Mom would've loved Acyn. You're in good hands and deeply loved." He squeezes me back.

After a moment, we let each other go. I sit next to Acyn, giving him a hug and kiss. "I love you."

"I love you too, Sunshine." He kisses me again. "May I?" he asks, motioning towards the box.

He takes it from my hand, gets down on one knee, and slides it on my finger. It fits me perfectly. I crash into him, hugging him so hard we both tumble to the floor. My dad laughs as I press a kiss to Acyn's lips before rolling on my back and holding my hand up to look at the ring again. It has a cushion cut diamond in the center with two smaller diamonds on the side and a gold band. I get up and give my dad another hug.

Grabbing my hand, he looks at the ring. "She would be so proud of you. I know it hasn't been easy with her not being here during this time, but know she's always with you." He kisses my hand before pulling me into another hug.

I wish I could say the loss of my mother hurts less with time, but there isn't a day I don't miss her. When major events happen in my life, her absence is only amplified. There are days the void is gaping, and I fear it'll swallow me whole. But I have my dad, Acyn, my supportive family and group of friends who hold me up and love me fiercely. I like to believe they were all handpicked by her and placed in my life exactly when I needed them. She may not be here, but her love for me transcends her death, and I feel it around me every day.

The next afternoon, my phone vibrates with a text from Marisa.

Marisa: On my way, babe! Can't wait for you to see everything.

Gloria insisted on me getting my rest instead of waking up early to help setup for the reception. With Ava in charge of the décor, I know she will bring what I wanted to life and make it better than I dreamt. Acyn and I had a lazy morning in bed, but we had to eventually get up to get him a new button down since I ruined his original one on our wedding night. I'll gladly take the blame and do it again. He's off to Greyson's house to get ready with the guys, and I'll be here at our house with the girls.

"What dress are you wearing today?" he asks with his tux bag slung over his shoulder before walking out the door.

"The one I wore for our wedding. I'm donating the other one to Brides for a Cause. Why?"

"Because I want to unwrap you again. There's something about that dress." He gives me a devilish grin.

Tugging on the collar of his shirt, I pull him towards me until his lips meet mine. "I look forward to it."

He kisses me again before pulling away and looking into my eyes, tucking a curl behind my ear. "I'll see you soon, Mrs. DeConto."

"That sounds so good coming from you and—" There's a knock at the door. It's probably for the best. We have a reception to get to. "I'll see you soon. Love you."

Opening the door, we're met by Marisa, Sevyn, and Quinn.

"Ladies and Sevyn." He nods as he steps around them.

"Excuse you, bro! Am I not a fucking lady?" Sevyn throws her hands up.

"You're lucky Zane married your crazy ass is all I'm gonna say." He smirks, dodging her punch.

"Alright, Harls! Let's get you glammed up," Marisa says, stepping inside and grabbing my hand.

A short while later, the girls have me feeling like a Queen. My kinky curls are in a simple half up, half down style with a floral gold accent barrette. Quinn has made it look effortless, with soft curls cascading down my back, even though we started the hairstyle last night. With kinky curls, sometimes they need to be stretched in order to achieve the desired look, and Quinn did just that. For my makeup, Marisa kept it natural with nude colors, a soft shimmer, and a hint of rose gold to give me a glowing, dewy look. Sevyn treated me earlier this week to getting my nails and toes done. My nails are almond-shaped with a nude base and rose gold foiling details.

Once I'm ready, the girls change into their dresses. It was hard for me to decide on a color scheme for the wedding. Instead, I decided I wanted rose gold accents. Their bridesmaid's dresses are rose gold satin with spaghetti straps and a cowl neck. All of them look stunning. It causes their warmly hued skin tones to look they're glowing. Raven arrives to take photos as we're gathering in the living room. I couldn't be surrounded by a better group of women. I'm not sure that I'd be where I'm standing without them. They've been there for and have helped me in countless ways. I'm grateful to be sharing this moment with them. It makes me teary-eyed, causing me to sniffle.

"No!" Quinn shouts, tipping her head back, fanning her face. "Do not start crying. My pregnancy hormones will have me bawling at the mere mention of tears."

"I'm sorry!" I laugh. "I can't help it." A tear rolls down my cheek.

"Cry away, babe! We didn't use waterproof makeup for nothing." Marisa says with tears in her eyes.

"You look gorgeous, and I know I've said it before, but I'm so happy you're my sister-in-law." Sevyn pulls me into a hug with tears in her eyes.

Raven is snapping pictures of us in our feelings, and it makes me laugh. I can't wait to see these pictures. I know without a doubt, one of them is getting framed. Someone's phone chimes. It turns out to be Sevyn's.

"Car service is here," she announces. "Are we ready?"

"Absolutely."

Sodo Park is a building with a rustic, elegant atmosphere. It's industrial, yet romantic. I felt it fit Acyn and me perfectly. The walls are brick with aged wood floors, and large wood columns line the length of the venue with white curtains hung whimsically between them. Wood beams criss cross the high ceiling, and natural light spills in from industrial style windows.

The soft warm glow of the halogen bulbs, hanging on string lights from the ceiling, give an enchanting look to the place. With Ava's touches, it looks like a scene from a fairy tale. While the venue provided most of the décor, Ava designed the accent pieces to make it unique for our reception. There's a floral arch, set up behind the bride and groom's table, made of sunflowers, champagne colored roses, white peonies, ranunculuses, and greenery. They made my waterfall style bouquet of the same mix.

They covered the guests' tables with white tablecloths and floral centerpieces. And of course, there's a designated space for our guests to take photos. It's decorated in the same floral mix as the arch behind our table. This is more beautiful than I imagined in my head. Seeing it with the unique details elevates this space even further. I didn't think that was possible, but I expect nothing less from Ava.

"Do you love it?" Sevyn asks. They all look at me expectantly.

Before I can answer, we're met by Gloria, Ava, and Acyn's two older sisters. All of them cry when they see me. I'm not sure what the point of wearing makeup today is.

"My dear, you are breathtaking," Gloria says, wrapping me in a hug.

"Thank you."

"We are so happy you're a part of our family now."

"Gloria, you're going to make me really cry."

"I truly am happy for you two." She kisses my cheek.

"Now that we live closer, hopefully we can get to know each other better." Annalise, Acyn's oldest sister, smiles at me.

"Yeah, welcome to the family," says Nora, his second oldest sister, giving me a tight hug.

His older sisters recently moved back to the area. They're connected at the hip, much like Acyn and Sevyn. It's interesting how that worked out. Maybe now that they're older, and the age gaps aren't as noticeable, the siblings will all become closer.

Ava is holding Mercy as she hugs me. I asked her to be a bridesmaid, too, and she looks stunning in her dress. Sevyn made Emery and Mercy's dresses so they could match the bridesmaid's dresses. The only difference is that they have cap sleeves with a square neck and a bow in the back.

"I know why Acyn wanted to marry you on the coast all by himself," she says low enough for only me to hear.

I toss my head back with laughter, but still feel the heat creep up my neck. "Ava!"

"What?" She shrugs with a smile. "I can't blame the man is all I'm saying."

I kiss Mercy on the cheek, and she lunges for me. Catching her, I pull her into my arms. "Mercy, you look like a princess." She giggles and pats her dress.

"Alright, little girl. Harlow has to go find her husband. You two are walking in together, right?" Ava takes Mercy from my arms.

"Yes." My heart skips a few beats. I saw him only a few hours ago, and you'd think it's been days with the way my body is buzzing with excitement.

"He should be on—"

Her sentence is cut short as he appears in the hallway with his entourage, and his eyes immediately find mine. He is so handsome it nearly hurts. Everyone else seems to fade away as he nears, wrapping his arm around my waist and pulling me towards him until our lips meet.

"Sunshine, you look more gorgeous with each passing day."

"I'm pretty damn lucky myself." I splay my hand across his chest and kiss him again.

Gloria embraces us both in a hug. "You two..." are the only words she can find as tears stream down her cheeks.

"Mom..." Acyn says, wiping them away.

"I'm just so happy for you both." She wipes her cheeks. "Okay." She takes a deep breath in an attempt to compose herself. "Felix will announce you two, and then you can come in."

"Sounds like a plan." I smile.

She leaves us alone again. I can hear the chatter and laughter of our nearest and dearest gathered in the reception area. I'm excited to spend the next few hours with them, celebrating our love. Acyn cups my face in his hand, holding me flush against his body as I look up into his eyes. He caresses my cheek, not saying a word as we look at each other. We stay like this until my dad saying our names pulls us from our moment.

"Ready, Mrs. DeConto?"

"Always, Mr. DeConto."

He interlaces his fingers with mine as we walk out to the cheers of our family and friends.

CHAPTER 17

Acyn

I was dreading the reception until I realized I get to be with the most gorgeous woman to walk this earth. I may be a little bias, but she's as close to heaven as I can get without dying. Everything about her is graceful from the way she walks, talks, and even how she snorts when she laughs. She makes everything near her glow a little brighter.

As I'm whispering something in Harlow's ear, I feel a tug on my suit jacket. I look down to see Emery, flower basket in tow, and her big brown eyes looking up at me.

"Uncle Ace, will you dance with me, please?"

Kneeling, I smile at her. "Of course, I'll dance with my favorite girl."

I've danced with her countless times tonight, but it's hard to say no to the twins. Yeah, I'm pretty much fucked when Harlow and I have kids. They'll want for nothing, and I can't wait to give them everything. I twirl Emery out onto the dance floor. She giggles as her dress spins out around her.

"Uncle Ace, will you bring me back a present when you leave on the airplane with Harlow?"

I chuckle. "What do you want?"

"A seashell. Like a mermaid."

"I think I can manage—"

"And pearls, too."

"Pearls?" I ask, raising a brow. "Did your mommy tell you to ask for those?"

She nods. "Mommy said go big or go home."

A chuckle resonates in my chest. "Figured. I will bring you back seashells." Looks like I can say no.

"Pinky promise?" She holds up her pinky.

Hooking mine with hers, I say, "Promise."

"Okay." She smiles, turning around and skipping off in the opposite direction.

And that's how you get finessed by a four-year-old. Harlow stands next to me as I watch Emery skip away.

"She looks happy."

"Yeah, once I promised to bring her back a gift, she was done with me. I'm pretty sure all those dances were to butter me up."

"Smart girl." She smirks.

I grab her hand, twirling her around, and pull her back into my arms. "Please tell me it's time to go."

She tosses her head back with laughter. "You've been a good sport. We can go. I'm sure they'll stay until the drinks run out."

"Thank fuck." I let out a sigh. I've reached my social quota for the next two weeks, maybe years. All I want is her.

We make our rounds, saying our goodbyes. My mom announces for everyone to gather outside for our farewell. Of course, we couldn't leave quietly. I've never seen my mom so proud of me in my life and it was something I needed to see after the choppy waters we were on. Minutes later, Harlow and I are walking through a tunnel of sparklers held out by our family and friends as they cheer us on, shouting well wishes.

A driver stands outside of the limo, holding the door open for us to slide in. She drapes her legs over mine as we settle into the seat, letting out a sigh.

"What's on your mind, Mrs. DeConto?"

"I don't know if I like Sunshine or Mrs. DeConto more." She simpers.

I chuckle. "Ready to have two uninterrupted weeks together?"

"I've been ready since you proposed," she says, giving me a look.

I already know what time it is. Without looking, my fingers find the button for the partition as she straddles me.

"You look like pure unadulterated sin in that suit."

I push her dress up, exposing her thighs as I caress them. "To match your energy, I've wanted to be inside you the moment I saw you in this dress."

Her lips crash into mine as she reaches down between us, unfastening my belt. Her hands are on a mission to get my dick out of my pants. Pulling it out, she strokes my length, causing my head to lull back. Her touch feels like ecstasy.

She raises her hips enough to pull her panties to the side. Her lips meet mine again as she slowly lowers herself onto me. She moans. It's one of my favorite sounds. I grip her ass cheeks as she bounces on my dick. This woman is everything. She leans back, giving me easier access to massage her clit. Her moans grow louder as she gets closer to the edge. I'm not sure if this partition is soundproof, but I don't care because the look on Harlow's face right now is one I aim to see daily. She bites her lip, and I can tell she's on the cusp of her release.

"Cum for me, Sunshine."

And she does. Her eyes lock onto mine as she unravels for me, crying out my name. One of her hands grabs the back of my neck and the other grasps my shoulder as she rides me to my release. I match her thrusts, gripping her hips and finding my release a few pumps later as I spill into her. Harlow doesn't stop riding me, though. She likes to make sure her pussy gets every drop.

Once she's satisfied, her hips stop moving, and she rests her forehead against mine.

"To think," she says breathlessly. "I get to be lost in you for a lifetime."

I rub my thumb along her bottom lip. "I've been lost in you since you gave me that first shitty cup of coffee."

She laughs. "This is how we're starting our honeymoon?"

"Nah, you started it by riding me like a professional jockey."

"Can you blame me, though?" She wraps her arms around my neck.

"Hell no." I kiss her. "You can ride me any time, any place."

We feel the limousine come to a stop. Greyson's gift to us is a private jet flight to and from the Seychelle islands, which is the only reason we're leaving immediately after the reception. Asher covered where we'll stay while there. I think it's safe to say we've got the best group of friends. I climb out of the limo first and hold my hand out to Harlow. She takes it, climbing out after me.

"Alright, Sunshine. Into forever."

It took us a day to recover from our travels. Flying privately was a luxury, but we were in the air for nearly two days. When we landed for the final time, I was tempted to kiss the earth. Even Harlow, who loves to travel, was happy to not have to board another plane. When we arrived, it was nighttime, and we didn't really see much. As soon as we got to the bungalow, we crashed.

Now that we've had an adequate amount of rest, we're walking the white sand beaches as the turquoise waves lap at our feet. The picturesque view and the smile on Harlow's face make the long trip worth it.

"Did you want to do something today?"

"No. This is all I wanted. To be here with you."

Our only plans are to rest, have sex, and be beach bums. I'd say we're doing a damn good job.

"Actually, maybe we can find a local place to eat... with proper food. I appreciate the butler, but foo foo fancy food doesn't really cut it for me."

"You don't like that shit either?" Being waited on hand and foot isn't all it's cracked up to be.

She bursts out laughing. "No! I was thinking it would be a more authentic Seychelles cuisine, but it's a little too fancy for my blood."

"I thought you liked it and I wasn't gonna spoil your enjoyment. But shit, let's go find some little hole in the wall, mom and pop place."

"Please, because I'm gonna starve between inadequate meals and marathon sex."

I scoop her up in my arms, and she squeals with laughter as I start toward the bungalow. "I can't have my wife starving."

After I got us lost, although I'll never admit that to Harlow, we pull up to the restaurant she found online. It's one of the highest rated and the trip gave us an opportunity to see the island in daylight. I'm not sure if it was me taking a wrong turn or Harlow having to stop to take pictures of everything along the way that took us so long to get here.

Regardless, we're here, and my stomach rumbles at the smell of the food coming from the restaurant. Although, it's not really a restaurant. There's only a window to order from and then there are various picnic areas near it. At this point, I think anything will be better than the food from where we're staying. We're only in the line for a few minutes before it's our turn.

"What can I get you?" the man asks.

"What do you recommend?" Harlow smiles, looking at the menu. "I want to fall in love with the food."

The guy smiles at her, and I don't miss the way his eyes take her in. "I think the food will fall in love with you."

Harlow tosses her head back with laughter. "A charmer."

"Let me know if it's working," he says. "I'll make you a plate of our best. How about that?"

"Sold." Harlow smiles as she steps to the side for me to order.

"What can I get you?" The man asks, all flirtatiousness gone.

"Mmm..." I say, pretending to study the menu. "I think I'll have... the same as my wife." I wrap my arm around Harlow's neck, pulling her toward me. The man is around our age and a little too fucking bold for my tastes.

Harlow leans into me as she giggles. "Calm down."

The man points the spoon at me, laughing. "I knew she was too pretty to be here alone. Let me guess, a honeymoon?"

"Yes!" Harlow says, holding her hand up to show him her ring.

"A very lucky man you are." He winks at me.

"I'm well aware." I kiss Harlow's temple

"The name is Michael, and you two are about to the eat the best food on this island." He smiles, resuming filling two Styrofoam containers with food.

A few minutes later, he hands us our containers. "What is it?" Harlow asks.

"Curry koko bernik, stir-fried squid, white rice, and papaya chutney."

"Squid?" Harlow asks, glancing down at that container with a look of uncertainty. I can't help but laugh at her.

"Try it." He reassures her. "You'll love it."

I pay him, and he tells us to visit again before we leave. I'm sure it's so he can see Harlow again. Flirty little fucker. If his food isn't good, I will let him know. But judging by the smell of it, it's going to be tasty.

"Not sure about the squid," she says, sitting down next to me at the picnic table.

"Live a little, Sunshine."

She pokes at what appears to be the squid with her plastic fork. I bite back a laugh. It takes her nearly a minute before she shovels some onto her fork and puts it into her mouth. She chews slowly before she lets out a moan.

"Ohhh my God!" she says with wide eyes. "Try it!"

Anytime she moans, I already know the food is going to be good. "I'm glad it is, because I would hate to have to fight your new friend."

She snorts with laughter. "So jealous for no reason."

I take a bite of food and want to shovel the rest of it into my mouth. "I have every reason to be with you."

Harlow smiles, resting her head on my shoulder, and then she digs into her food. When we finish, we order more to take back with us so we don't have to rely on the food the butler is trying to kill us with. We'll definitely have to figure something out with that, but this will do for now.

When we arrive back at our place, the sun is setting. Harlow grabs some blankets she somehow found on an island that is known for its perpetual summer.

"Let's watch the sunset."

I'm not gonna say no. I just follow her. Once on the beach, she settles between my legs, and I wrap my arms around her.

"Acyn..." she says after a few minutes of listening to the waves.

"Yeah, Sunshine?"

"You make me so fucking happy. I just needed you to know that."

I kiss the top of her head. "You've been lighting up my world since I met you with that brilliant smile and shitty cup of coffee."

"Fuck you." She laughs. "What if someone else told me I made shitty cups of coffee?"

"They would be forced to apologize and then suffer from burns because of the coffee I'd throw at them."

"But it's okay for you?" She snorts with laughter.

"Yes." I shrug. "Always has been. Always will be."

"You know... you're a jerk. But you're my jerk."

I let out a rumble of laughter before tipping her back and claiming her mouth. Her laughs quickly turn to moans.

"I'll be right back. My phone's ringing," I say to Harlow through the bathroom door.

Sevyn's name flashes across the screen. When I pick up, I'm met by Eli's little face.

"Uncle Ace..." he whispers.

"Eli." I chuckle. "Are you supposed to—"

"Hey! Who are you talking to, sir?" I hear Sevyn ask in the background. The phone clatters to the floor, followed by Eli's giggles and running feet.

Sevyn appears a few seconds later. "Oh, it's you." She smiles. "I'm surprised you answered and aren't balls deep in Harlow right now."

"For fuck's sake, Sevyn." I laugh.

"What? I've caught you two in the act before. I'm not new to this."

"Totally worth it. No regrets."

"So... why the fuck are you on the phone with your little sister?"

"Harlow's been sick today. I'm not sure what's going on."

"Did she drink the water?"

"Nope."

"It's probably something she ate. Maybe she got food poisoning."

"Nah." I shake my head. "I don't think it's that. We've had the same food. But she's been puking since she woke up."

She smiles. "Is she pregnant?"

"I—well... it's a possibility. She hasn't been on birth control and—fuckkkk, you're probably right."

"Is this a bad thing?" she asks.

"No. Hell, no. It would be the best thing. But Harlow thinks she has a bad case of food poisoning or something."

"Aw... bless her delusion." Sevyn snickers.

I hear the bathroom door open. "Aye, I gotta go. I'll talk to you when I get back."

"When you get back? I wanna know if she's pregnant now!"

"Gotta go, sis! Love ya." I hang up on her.

Harlow lays down on the bed, covering her eyes with her forearm. "Who was that?"

"Sevyn. Actually, it was Eli, but Sevyn caught him and took the phone."

She chuckles. "It was probably about their gifts."

"Yep..." My voice trails off as I stare at her.

She removes her arm from her eyes to peek at me. "What? Why are you looking at me like that? Do I have puke on me?"

"No... it's just that—do you think you could be pregnant... maybe?"

She stares up at the canopy draped over the bed. "Um..." she sits up, pressing her fingers to her mouth. For a moment I think she gonna puke again, but her eyes meet mine.

Her eyes widen as she gasps. "Acyn... I think I'm pregnant."

The look on her face is priceless. It's a mix of shock and wonder.

"Do you want to see if we can find a test? Or we can wait until after the honeymoon."

"Wait?" She slides off the bed. "Can you wait that long?"

"Fuck no, but I didn't want to sound pushy."

"Let's go find one then," she says with laughter. "I'm nervous now."

"Why? You'll be a great mom?"

"I don't know." She shrugs, slipping on her sandals. "I knew it would happen eventually with me not being on birth control anymore, but when it didn't happen the first few months... I kind of forgot about it. Well, until someone mentioned us having kids. I don't know. I wondered if we'd have kids or not. I put it out of mind instead of being hopeful, you know?"

I caress her cheek. "I didn't know you felt that way. You can always talk to me about anything, and I'll listen."

"I know." She kisses me. "And I'm grateful for that."

"Let's go see if you're knocked up or not."

"Knocked up?" She cackles. "Really?"

"Let's see if you're with child. Is that better?"

"No." She shakes her head as we walk out to the car. "That doesn't sound like you. Surprisingly, knocked up does, though."

"Of course, it does." I chuckle, shutting the door once she sits in the seat.

After a trip to the store, I'm sitting on the edge of the tub, waiting for her to pee on the pregnancy test.

"If it says I'm not pregnant, I'll probably cry. I thought of at least," she holds the stick between her legs, "fifty names. And," she pees, "I already have a vision of what their room would look like. The baby will be close in age with Kyrell and Quinn's baby, too."

"You thought of a hell of a lot in such a short time." I chuckle.

She places the cap on the end of the stick before washing her hands and flushing the toilet. "You're ready for a baby, right?"

"I'm ready for everything with you."

She kisses me. "And now we wait."

I realize my patience has its limits as we wait for the test to tell us if we're going to be parents or not.

"Check it." Harlow rests her chin on my shoulder as I reach for the test sitting on the edge of the sink. She looks away when I look at it.

"Sunshine," I put my arm around her shoulders, pulling her close to me, and hold it up in front of her face. "Look."

She looks at the test, then at me, and then back at the test. "I'm knocked up!" she squeals, grinning as she wraps her arms tightly around me.

When she pulls away, I pull her back to me and bring her lips to mine. This woman, wrapped up in my arms, has given me everything she possibly could. Her time, friendship, trust, love, soul, mind, heart...

every single thing she's willingly entrusted to me. I pick her up and she wraps her legs around me. My lips don't leave hers as I take her to the room. I need to feel her on me in every way. We're tangled as we crash onto the bed.

I reluctantly pull away from her to take off my jeans and t-shirt. She slides the straps of her sundress off her shoulders, pulling her arms out. I drag it down her body until it's sliding off her thighs, and she's fully exposed. I kiss her neck, grazing her skin with my teeth before sucking it into my mouth. Her hand grasps my length as she lines me up with her center. She gasps as I push into her. I watch as her eyes close and she bites down on her lip, taking every inch of me into her. My body shudders with the pleasure of her being wrapped around me.

"Harlow, look at me." I press a kiss to her lips as her eyes slowly open and look into mine. "You have my soul, Sunshine."

"Acyn..." she lets out a breathy moan as I move inside her.

She hooks one leg around my waist and the other she places over my shoulder, allowing me to plunge into her. I grip her ankle as I sit up, watching her breasts bounce and my dick slide in and out of her. She brings her hand down between us until her fingers are on her clit. I groan as I watch her massage herself. I love watching her. Heat pricks my skin as I feel the release I only find in her building in my core.

Harlow's breathing is ragged as she nears her climax. She's rubbing her clit faster, harder as she cries out with pleasure. Her eyes snap open, locking onto mine as her pussy tightens around my dick as she cums for me.

"Goddamn," I grunt. "You're so fucking tight."

She opens her legs wider for me. I grip her hips and thrust into her as she kneads her breasts and rubs her nipples. The sight of her beneath me, open for me, is my undoing. My release rips through me, causing my body to shake with pleasure as my hips stutter and breath hitches. I pump every drop into her, completely satisfied. She closes her eyes with a smile on her face, letting her body go limp. I collapse beside her and pull her into my arms.

"Can't believe you're knocked up." I chuckle and she bursts out laughing.

CHAPTER 18

Harlow

L ater that day, we find ourselves on the beach, ready to watch another sunset. We spent the afternoon in a tangled mess of limbs. I'd still prefer to be naked and wrapped up in his arms, but we had to eat and to be honest, the sunsets are worth watching every day here. I relax on the blanket next to Acyn, resting my head on his shoulder, enjoying the warm breeze brushing past our skin and the sound of the ocean waves kissing the shore.

"Are we announcing this now or later?"

I sit up, getting a better look at him. "You want to announce it now?"

"Hell, yeah." he says, splaying his hand across my stomach. "Unless you don't want to."

"No, no. I do. You rarely willingly want to share personal things with people."

"Yeah, but I want everyone to know we're having a baby." He pulls me onto his lap.

"Your excitement is so damn cute." I kiss him. "Let's tell everyone then. But I think we should tell our parents first."

"Yeah." He nods. "My mom would kill me if she had to find out online.

I toss my head back with laughter. "She would."

The call back home to our parents is short, as it's much later there. I thought Gloria was going to faint from excitement. Our dads are much calmer, but there wasn't a dry eye. I realize we'll be lucky if we get to hold our own child after they're born.

When we hang up, I pull the tripod out of my bag and set it up in the sand. The vibrant turquoise ocean and setting sun will be our backdrop. I'm wearing a barely there, fluorescent yellow bikini and Acyn, to my pleasure, is shirtless, wearing black swim trunks. He brushes the curls out of my face that were swept up by the wind.

"Ready?" I ask, straddling his lap.

He presses a kiss to my stomach before looking up at me, and I tangle my fingers in his curls. Sitting on his lap, I bring my lips to his, dipping my tongue into his mouth as we get lost in the bliss.

"Let me turn off the camera before we make a movie."

"I'm not opposed," he says, with his hands palming my ass.

"Of course not," I smirk. "You live for the thrill." I scroll through the pictures.

"Do you have—"

I press a finger to his lips. "Did you not just say you wanted to announce this with a picture?"

"Yes, I did," he says. "But—" I raise a brow "—take your time, Sunshine."

I snort with laughter as he swallows his words of protest. I hand him my phone. "Pick one or some. I can never decide."

Within seconds, he says, "this one."

I peer at the screen. "That's my favorite, too." He's kissing my stomach, my hands are in his hair, and I have the biggest smile on my face. The setting sun gives the illusion the water is glittering behind us.

"And these two," he adds, showing me. The second one is of him looking up at me, and there's a look of undeniable happiness on our faces. The final picture is of us in silhouette, kissing with the sun setting behind us.

"Perfect." I smile at him. His phone chimes a few seconds later and I hand it to him. "We'll upload at the same time. What should the caption be?"

I watch as he adds the caption 'knocked up'. He laughs as he does it, and I giggle as I type out the same.

"Alright, let's put it out there, Sunshine."

We hit the check at the same time. Not even thirty seconds later, our phones chime with notifications. I grab his phone, powering both of them off, and toss them to the side.

I wrap my arms around his neck. "It's out there. We'll talk about it with everyone else when we get back. Now, where were we?"

"Exactly where we want to be," he says, pulling me on top of him as my lips crash into his.

Our happy ending isn't really an ending, it's only the beginning of forever.

THANK YOU

Thank you for reading! If you enjoyed this novel, please consider leaving a review on Amazon and Goodreads so other readers can enjoy it, too!

Keep in touch with me. Subscribe to my newsletter and follow me on social media to be the first to know about new releases, giveaways, freebies, and more!

Made in the USA
Las Vegas, NV
02 October 2023